COLD SHADOWS

ELLIE JORDAN, GHOST TRAPPER, BOOK TWO

by

J.L. Bryan

Published 2014
JLBryanbooks.com

Copyright 2014 J.L. Bryan

All rights reserved.

This book or any portion thereof may not be reproduced or used in any manner whatsoever without the express written permission of the publisher except for the use of brief quotations in a book review.

All characters appearing in this work are fictitious. Any resemblance to real persons, living or dead, is purely coincidental.

ISBN-10: 1503028496
ISBN-13: 978-1503028494

Acknowledgments

I appreciate everyone who has helped with this book. Several authors beta read it for me, including Daniel Arenson, Alexia Purdy, Robert Duperre, and Michelle Muto. The final proofing was done by Thelia Kelly. The cover is by PhatPuppy Art.

Most of all, I appreciate the book bloggers and readers who keep coming back for more! The book bloggers who've supported me over the years include Danny, Heather, and Heather from Bewitched Bookworks; Mandy from I Read Indie; Michelle from Much Loved Books; Shirley from Creative Deeds; Katie and Krisha from Inkk Reviews; Lori from Contagious Reads; Heather from Buried in Books; Kristina from Ladybug Storytime; Chandra from Unabridged Bookshelf; Kelly from Reading the Paranormal; AimeeKay from Reviews from My First Reads Shelf and Melissa from Books and Things; Kristin from Blood, Sweat, and Books; Lauren from Lose Time Reading; Kat from Aussie Zombie; Andra from Unabridged Andralyn; Jennifer from A Tale of Many Reviews; Giselle from Xpresso Reads; Ashley from Bookish Brunette; Loretta from Between the Pages; Ashley from Bibliophile's Corner; Lili from Lili Lost in a Book; Line from Moonstar's Fantasy World; Lindsay from The Violet Hour; Rebecca from Bending the Spine; Holly from Geek Glitter; Louise from Nerdette Reviews; Isalys from Book Soulmates; Jennifer from The Feminist Fairy; Heidi from Rainy Day Ramblings; Kristilyn from Reading in Winter; Kelsey from Kelsey's Cluttered Bookshelf; Lizzy from Lizzy's Dark Fiction; Shanon from Escaping with Fiction; Savannah from Books with Bite; Tara from Basically Books; Toni from My Book Addiction; and anyone else I missed!

For John and Judy

Also by J.L. Bryan:

The Ellie Jordan, Ghost Trapper series
Ellie Jordan, Ghost Trapper
Cold Shadows
The Crawling Darkness

The Jenny Pox series (supernatural/horror)
Jenny Pox
Tommy Nightmare
Alexander Death
Jenny Plague-Bringer

Urban Fantasy/Horror
Inferno Park
The Unseen

Science Fiction Novels
Nomad
Helix

The Songs of Magic Series (YA/Fantasy)
Fairy Metal Thunder
Fairy Blues
Fairystruck
Fairyland
Fairyvision
Fairy Luck

Chapter One

"That's where the bodies are buried," Stacey said, pointing to the low, swampy depression in the center of the back yard. It looked like it was still flooded from yesterday's rain.

"What bodies?" I asked. I parked behind a tan Jeep Patriot, a surprisingly cheap car if it belonged to the owner of this big old Georgian mansion. The house had a symmetrical, well-kept face, but the sides and back were closer to ruin, with missing and broken shutters and mold growing between the bricks. It was as if the graceful front of the house were nothing more than a mask of rationality and order, disguising decay and incipient madness beneath.

"The bodies of the restless ghosts, duh," Stacey said.

"We haven't even determined whether this house is haunted, Stacey." The driveway was uncomfortably narrow, barely wide enough for our cargo van.

"I'm just taking early bets. Twenty bucks on us eventually finding dead bodies there. Who'll take me on that?" Stacey glanced into the back of the van, as if somebody else were sitting there. She smiled, kind of suddenly. "So...when do you think we'll call Jacob in on this one?"

"I hope the case won't be difficult enough to require psychic help," I said, and her smile fell. "Psychics never come to the initial consultation, anyway."

"Never?" This seemed to disappoint her somehow. "Why not?"

"Because they're not supposed to have any details of the case. They go in with a blank slate, with as little information as possible."

"Don't you think psychics are fascinating, though?" Stacey asked.

"Not really. Their results are usually pretty mixed."

"So...when *would* we call Jacob, theoretically?"

"You know, you can just call him if you want," I said. "It doesn't have to be about work."

"Then what would my excuse be?" Stacey asked. I think she'd developed a crush on Jacob Weiss right around the time he saved us from a horde of attacking ghosts. He was a reluctant psychic, his powers awoken after he'd nearly died in a plane crash. Jacob didn't mainly think of himself as a psychic medium. He mainly thought of himself as an up-and-coming young accountant at a CPA firm downtown, who happened to speak with the dead in his spare time because *they* wouldn't stop talking to *him*. It was just therapy for him, learning to cope with his unwanted new abilities.

Jacob was reasonably cute, if you forced me to have an opinion, and he also dressed pretty well, which probably scored him a lot of points with Stacey.

"We'd better introduce ourselves before our clients start wondering about the weird van in their driveway," I said.

A man sat painting at an easel on the brick patio behind the house, but he apparently hadn't noticed us. A straw hat shaded his head, and he wore headphones. He was hefty, badly overweight, maybe in his thirties or forties.

Stacey and I climbed out, me with my black toolbox of basic ghost-hunting gear, Stacey with her camera bag slung over her shoulder. I was the lead investigator and Stacey was the tech manager, my assistant. She'd only been with Eckhart Investigations for about eight weeks, since graduating from the College of Art and Design with her film degree. I'd been working with Calvin Eckhart for almost eight years, having foisted myself onto him as an unwanted apprentice during my freshman year of college.

A ghost killed my parents when I was fifteen, a nasty pyrokinetic monster named Anton Clay. Calvin was still a homicide detective with the city police, and he'd unraveled the case for me—it wasn't the first time he'd encountered dangerous ghosts around the ridiculously haunted city of Savannah. I'd stuck with him since he retired and opened the agency, because I'm determined to protect the living against the dead.

Stacey and I strolled up the brick walkway past garden plots that alternated between thriving blossoms and dead yellow stalks, as if the irrigation and the automatic sprinklers weren't functioning so well. Thin marble columns framed the front door, supporting a little half-circle balcony with a wrought-iron railing on the second floor.

I climbed the brick steps under the shade of the balcony above. The tall door was painted a cheerful white, matching the window trim all over the house.

I rang the doorbell.

The woman who answered was short, round-faced and chubby, with an earnest look in her brown eyes. She wore a pastel purple blouse and pinstriped pantsuit bottoms.

"Yes?" she asked, glancing between us.

"Hi, I'm Ellie Jordan, from Eckhart Investigations," I said. "Are you Mrs. Paulding?"

"Thank the Lord." She breathed out a slow sigh, as if our presence alone removed some kind of long-suffered weight off her back, and ushered us inside. "Y'all want some sweet tea? Chex mix?"

"No, thank you, ma'am." I followed her into the entrance hall, which was tall and ran all the way to the back of the house, but was also narrow and cluttered with furniture. A squarish staircase with three flights wrapped around the very back of the hall, above a pair of glass doors that led into the back yard.

Polished antique sofas, chairs, and lamp tables lined the walls, under assorted landscape and seascape paintings in heavy, dark wooden frames that seemed more suited to portraits of notable dead ancestors.

Despite the big twelve-pane windows at each end of the hall, it was gloomy, and the dark air felt heavy on my skin. The place already felt haunted to me, but I don't go by my feelings. I'm an evidence-and-empiricism kind of girl. As far as this line of work allows, anyway.

"This is such a beautiful house!" Stacey gushed. "How old is it?"

"They say it was built in 1841," Mrs. Paulding replied. "Some of the furniture's even older, I guess."

"Mind if I take some video?" Stacey asked, unzipping her camera bag.

"If you have to," the woman said. "The place looks a sight. Well, it always does, to tell you the truth."

"Mrs. Paulding, this is our tech manager, Stacey Ray Tolbert," I said.

"Just call me Stacey!" Stacey gave her an enthusiastic handshake, which seemed to startle the woman.

"And you can call me Toolie," Mrs. Paulding said. "That's short for Theodora, but nobody's called me that since Momma died. Come on back, Gordon will want to see you. That's my husband." Her voice dropped to a whisper. "He has some breathing problems, just so you know."

As we followed her down the hall, I glanced through an archway into a family sitting room, furnished with more antique sofas, plus one big La-Z-Boy recliner aimed at the big-screen TV. The walls here were decorated along a sort of pop-art theme, I guess you'd call it, bright paintings depicting candies with names I didn't recognize—Munchmallows, Nickel Naks, Fizzy Lizzys. The only ones I did recognize were Pink Fairy cupcakes, which my mom had occasionally included in my school lunchbox as a cellophane-wrapped treat.

I noted some family pictures on the wall. The Pauldings were a family of four, their daughter a few years older than their son. The husband looked like a virile man, bearded and tanned in the family beach pictures.

We stepped out onto the rear patio, where the man we'd seen earlier was still painting. He still wore his headphones, and from this angle, I could see the portable oxygen tank by his feet, the tube running up toward his face.

"Gord!" Toolie Paulding tapped her husband's shoulder, startling him. He was painting an old-fashioned candy tin, similar to those in the living room. This one advertised COCO-MARSHIES! and the candy's mascot, which dominated the lid of the tin, was a creepy-looking ventriloquist's dummy in overalls and a straw hat, waving one arm and giving a gaping smile.

A color picture of the original tin, printed on regular paper, was attached to the side of the easel with a clothespin. It looked like he was using it for reference.

Gord, as she apparently called him, turned to look at us with an uncertain smile under the plastic tubing that fed oxygen into his nose. Never mind the living room photos of the virile man at the beach—he was pale, overweight, his beard scraggly and graying. He moved slowly.

"These are the ghost detectives, Ellie and Stacey," she told him, while helping him remove his headphones. "Ladies, this my husband

Gord."

"Very nice to meet you, sir," I said.

"Nice...to meet you," he replied, with a long gap to draw extra air. Stacey and I shook his hand gently.

Toolie invited us to sit on the deck chairs.

"So what can you tell us about your problems?" I asked. I took out a legal pad and a digital voice recorder.

"Where to begin?" Toolie brushed her hand through her hair, shaking her head.

"How long have you lived in this house?" I asked.

"Oh...two years, a little more?" Toolie said. "It actually belongs to my cousin Mary, but she said we could live here rent-free as long as we maintained and repaired it."

"That sounds awfully nice of her," I said. *Unless she knew the place was haunted*, I thought. "Does she live here in town?"

"Oh, no, she's lived over in Beaufort for several years," Toolie said, referring to a pretty ritzy beachside town over in South Carolina. "She inherited this house from her family—the other side of her family, obviously. Nobody in *my* family ever had a spare mansion to worry about." Toolie chuckled.

"Can you give us your cousin's contact information?" I asked. She was an obvious source for background information.

"I'd rather not," Toolie said, frowning suddenly. "When I've asked her, she says she doesn't know anything funny about the house. If you go talking to her, it might upset her...and we can't afford for her to get sore and throw us out..."

"I understand, ma'am. Where did you live before this house?"

"Just outside Raleigh, North Carolina," Toolie said. "The move meant Gord would have to travel a little further for work, but he was always traveling anyway. He was a sales and relationship representative for Pink Fairy Bakery. You know, the cupcakes?"

"Sure," I said. "I saw the paintings inside. They're really good." It never hurts to compliment the client. Besides, I kind of liked the old-fashioned candy boxes he'd painted. Wouldn't mind hanging one in my apartment, actually.

"Thank you," Gord said. "I started out painting...what I sold. Cupcakes. Chocolate Wands. Sparkle Wheels." He paused to breathe some more. "Then I got interested in vintage candies. Brands nobody...remembers." He gestured at his work in progress, the *Coco-Marshies!* tin with the creepy puppet.

"That's really neat," Stacey said, smiling at him.

"Gord has to paint outside now, because of the fumes," Toolie said. "It's a shame. We'd just set up a nice studio for him upstairs, and then he got sick."

"Do you mind if I ask...?" I asked.

"Emphysema," Toolie said. "*Severe* emphysema. He had to go on disability."

Gord scowled a little, as if he didn't appreciate her sharing this information.

"Did that begin before you moved here, or afterward?" I asked.

"A few months after we moved," Toolie said. "Gord used to smoke, but he quit ten years ago."

"Ten years?" Stacey asked. "That's not fair! He quit for ten years and then he gets sick from it--"

I gently motioned for Stacey to shut up, and she closed her mouth.

"Sorry," Stacey mumbled.

"The doctors can't figure out the cause," Toolie said. "Breathing just started to get difficult for him one day, like his lungs were drowning." Her mouth wavered, and for a second she looked like she would cry, but she forced herself to smile instead. She patted his arm.

Gord looked at the patio's brick floor tiles, as if ashamed of himself for getting sick. I felt sorry for him.

"Do you work?" I asked Toolie.

"Oh, yes. I used to be a sales associate at Napmaster Outlet back home. After we moved here, I got a job managing the Sir Sleepmore Mattresses by the mall. Everything was looking up at first, with the new job and this amazing old house, and I thought it would be nice for the kids to live here..." She frowned.

"How many kids do you have?" I asked, though I was pretty sure I knew the answer.

"Two. There's Juniper—she's thirteen now—and Crane, who's about to have his eighth birthday. The time goes by so fast. One minute, they're babies, and then they're rushing toward adulthood."

"How did they adjust to living here?" I asked.

"Well, it was good...at first. Then the strange things started happening."

Here we go. "Can you tell us what you and your family have experienced?"

"It started with small things—so small I blamed them on the

kids, to tell you the truth. My keys would be missing, and I'd find them somewhere strange, like on the stairs or at the bottom of the kitchen sink. Or a faucet would be left running. Don't even get me started on those plumbing problems! We had moaning, banging pipes, and we've had three plumbers out here to fix them. One changed out the the master valve, another installed a water hammer arrestor, but the problem kept coming back.

"In fact, the more the plumbers worked, the more trouble we had. We'd wake up and find water damage in the walls or a leaking pipe in the basement. Then it got strange—ceilings would leak in spots where there weren't any pipes. They couldn't find where the water was coming from, and half the time the spot would be all dried up before the plumber even arrived."

"That sounds stressful," I said.

"And expensive!" Toolie said. "The yard started to go to all-heck around then, too. The sprinkler system's always breaking down, and we can't seem to drain the low spot there..." She pointed to the pool of swampy, greenish water that had collected in the depression in her back lawn. "The rainwater just sits and sits. We hired a landscaper to make a little drainage pipe for it, but mud clogs it up so fast, it's just about useless."

Stacey snapped some pictures of the swampy yard. A small cottage sat in the rear corner of the lawn, built in imitation of the main house—brick with white trim, the two windows and the front door a perfect match with the features on the front of the mansion.

"What's that building?" I asked.

"Just an old shed," Toolie said. "We keep the lawn mower in there. It's mainly the yard man who uses it. I don't like going in there."

"Why not?"

"Too many spiders."

"Have there been any other events, or is it all water-related?" I asked.

"Oh, goodness, where to begin?" Toolie shook her head. "The first time I *knew* we had something strange in our house was when I was mixing up a pitcher of iced tea, right around Christmas. I was in the kitchen alone. I turned my back for one second, to fetch a lemon from the fridge, and something went *whap!* Well, I looked back to see my pitcher flying to the floor, spilling out the tea everywhere, just like someone had come along and knocked it off the counter. I was lucky it was the Tupperware and not my good glass pitcher."

"Is there any way it could have fallen on its own?" I asked. "Was it close to the edge? Sometimes, the condensation can make the counter slick--"

"No, no!" Toolie said. "It was moving fast, like somebody hit it."

"That must have been scary."

"Oh, yes."

"Have you ever seen anything else like that happen in this house?" I asked.

"Of course. Chairs slide, doors slam, clothes fly out of the closets..." Toolie shook her head. "It's been going on for months now."

"It knocked over my....easel," Gord said. "One time. Paints spilled all over...the bricks. I've seen it...move things around the house."

"So many things have happened, I don't know where to begin," Toolie said. "And the kids have seen things, too, especially Junie."

"Maybe it would help organize your thoughts if you showed us around the house," I said. "Then we can identify any possible paranormal hotspots."

"*Hauntspots*, we call them," Stacey added with a grin. That wasn't true. We'd never called them that, but I guessed Stacey would make it a point to use that word in the future, now that she'd gone and coined it.

"I'll...wait here," Gord said. "Want to finish...painting."

"It's looking really good," I told him. He smiled after us as Stacey and I followed Toolie back into the high, narrow central hall that bisected the house.

"I didn't want to say it in front of Gord," Toolie whispered after closing the door. "But I've seen it."

"What did you see?" I asked. I was pretty sure she meant an apparition, but I try not to ask leading questions.

"The ghost." Toolie glanced down the hall and up the stairs. I could hear something like thumping and screeching from the second floor. "Never mind that, it's just Juniper's music. She's in that teen rebel phase. Sounds scary, doesn't it?"

I nodded. "Where did you see the ghost?"

"In the craft room upstairs," Toolie said. "Listen, can y'all really get rid of ghosts?"

"In most cases, yes," I told her.

"Good. Cause I can't live in this house with this thing for one more day. I've had about enough."

"Do you feel like your family is in danger?" I asked.

"Heck, yes," Toolie said. "If it can throw furniture around, then it can throw us around, too."

Then she led us into the spacious living room to tell us more about her ghosts.

Chapter Two

The living room, though enormous, was cluttered with too many antique chairs, tables, cabinets, and hutches, making it difficult to navigate. The walls were paneled in light blond wood, and the ceiling was fourteen feet above us, trimmed in thick but simple molding. A pair of tall windows looked out on the back yard, through sheer curtains that dampened the bright sunlight. Pilasters flanked the broad brick fireplace.

I noticed a giant, greenish stain on the ceiling, not far from the slowly revolving ceiling fan. Whatever had dripped down from the ceiling hadn't exactly been Crystal Springs water. It was the color of slime topped with scum. Stacey took a picture.

"Was that one of the leaks you were talking about?" I asked.

"Oh, yes. There's no pipes up there to cause any leaks," Toolie said. "But that's not all that's happened in this room. The ghost's been very busy down here." She opened a door in a dark oaken cupboard, revealing a stack of board games. They had *Monopoly*, *Candy Land*, *Risk*, *Clue*, and a few other classics. "One night, I heard a ruckus down here about two in the morning. I found all these games pulled out, all over the floor. All mixed together. You had the *Risk* cannons rolling across *Candy Land*, the candlestick and revolver from

Clue stuck into that red-nosed guy from the *Operation* game, the Community Chest cards scattered from here all the way to the windows."

"You're sure it wasn't one of your kids?" I asked.

"Crane was sleeping over at a friend's house," she said. "Juniper said she didn't do it, and why would she, anyway? She was up in her room, playing video games with her headphones on."

I nodded, but the thirteen-year-old girl still sounded like a possible suspect to me.

"Anything else?" I asked.

"We'll find the couch cushions all over the floor when nobody's been in here. And the pictures! Look, it did it again!" Toolie gestured at a heavy mahogany end table full of framed pictures, mostly of their immediate family members, along with a few other people I assumed to be relatives or friends. Two of them were turned backward, facing the wall.

Toolie turned the pictures to face front again. Both were of her daughter Juniper, one in an elementary-school cheerleader uniform when she was six or seven years old, and another one showing her at ten or eleven, with braces, posed with a fist tucked under her chin. Like her mother, the girl had long brown hair and was a little pudgy. She looked like a friendly kid.

"It moves the pictures?" I asked.

"Oh, yes. Some mornings, they'll all be turned around, or they'll be lying flat like somebody came and slapped them over in the night. It's one of the things I used to blame on the kids, before I saw it for myself."

"You saw the pictures move?"

"They do it when my back's turned," Toolie said. "But I'll hear it. And I'll be the only one in the room. Oh, and sometimes this T.V. turns on late at night, all by itself, and I have to come switch it off." She gestured at the flatscreen on the wall. "Before that, it was the phonograph. It's hand-cranked, so how could it go on by accident?"

"Can I see the phonograph?"

Toolie led me toward a reddish wooden cabinet with a crank built into the side and a thick layer of dust on the engraved lid. She raised the lid to show me the turntable within.

"We never use this thing," Toolie said. "But the ghost does."

"It plays records?" I asked.

"It used to, until it figured out how to work the TV." Toolie shook her head and opened a drawer at the base of the cabinet, full of records dating back to the 1910's, their paper wrappers yellowed and crumbling. "We'd hear this scratchy music in the middle of the night and have to come cut it off. Always these old records, this big-band stuff. It happened a few times. It stopped after the T.V went to flipping itself on instead."

"And you're sure none of this is done by the kids?" I asked.

"Not after the other things I've seen. And not after that night I came here and saw the T.V. switching channels all by itself, just clicking through one after another. I turned it off, but I didn't tell nobody about it. Not for a while."

"What else have you seen in here?"

"That's the main things that have happened." Toolie led us through the open double doors into a small library, the shelves crammed full of old volumes and small statues. Leather-upholstered chairs flanked the little brick fireplace, and a thickly piled ornate rug covered most of the hardwood floor. "Books sometimes fly off the shelves. Makes a racket."

The library ceiling had two large, green stains, and the rug below it was discolored in the same areas.

"More of the strange leaks from nonexistent pipes?" I asked, and Toolie nodded.

The next set of double doors was closed—each room in the house seemed connected to the next by these double doors, but most of them were propped open like window shutters.

Toolie opened one door, but didn't step through.

"This is a guest room, but Gord's been sleeping here. The stairs are so hard on him."

The room was crammed full of more antique tables and chairs, plus a four-poster bed with thick, dark columns of cherry wood.

"Does anything happen in there?" I asked.

"Sure. Things move. And the ceiling." She pointed to more of the ugly green splotches. "Oh, but the biggest thing to happen on this floor was the dining room." Toolie led us up the central hall to the long, tall room, lit by a row of high windows. An open pair of double doors led into the kitchen beyond.

The polished birch table could have seated twelve. A large copper and crystal chandelier hung above the table, and paintings adorned the walls, featuring men and women in fancy dress wear of the nineteenth century.

"One time we were having supper in here," Toolie said. "We usually eat in the kitchen, but it was my husband's birthday, so I was trying to do something nice, have a nice family meal together. Right in the middle of supper, all the paintings come crashing down off the walls. Some of the plates and things jumped right off the table and hit the floor. Smashed the china gravy boat to pieces—I haven't mentioned that to my cousin. The china came with the house."

"Everybody was sitting down?" I asked. "There was nobody out of the room, nobody else in the house?"

"Well, Juniper, she was running out the door in a huff," Toolie said. "But she wasn't nowhere near the paintings. And her plate jumped off the table, her silverware, along with the gravy boat and mashed potatoes. She was out in the hall by the time that happened."

"Why was she running out?"

"Oh, she was upset about this boy...I guess it's her boyfriend, but I don't like to call him that. Dayton. He's fifteen, for one thing, two years older than her and goes to high school, and Junie's just going into the eighth grade in the fall. And he dresses like a thug, wears his sunglasses indoors, and he always smells like cigarettes. I mean, he's a bad kid."

"So you were fighting about her boyfriend?" I asked.

"Well, we was trying to tell her...again...that she wasn't allowed to see him." Toolie shook her head. "I knew supper was ruined as soon as we started talking about that boy."

Stacey and I shared a look. We were probably thinking the same thing.

"What is it?" Toolie asked.

"Sometimes, when you have a young person, especially an adolescent girl, and there's drama and stress, along with psychokinetic activity, objects moving by themselves...it's not actually a ghost," I said. "It's a poltergeist."

"Poltergeist!" Toolie's eyes widened. "Like in the movies?"

"Sort of," I said. "A poltergeist is created by a living person, usually a young person or child. It's not created intentionally. Their emotions can create a psychic discharge, if that makes sense."

"It doesn't, really." Toolie scratched her head.

"It's like a ghost, but of a living person instead of a dead one," I said. "It's usually destructive, lashing out with all the feelings that person is suppressing. Anger, frustration, sometimes grief."

"Wait, now. You're telling me Juniper made this poltergeist? She's the one who's haunting this house?"

"That's just one possibility," I said. "But from your description, it's something we have to consider. Have there been any other incidents with your daughter?"

"She says things move around in her room all the time," Toolie replied. "Of course, I didn't believe her at first."

"Can we speak to her?"

"Come on up." Toolie led us to the staircase, with three short flights that wrapped around the back end of the hall in a squarish spiral shape. The sound of angry industrial music grew louder as we climbed.

The stairs brought us to the upstairs hall, which had the same narrow, cluttered-with-furniture feeling as the one downstairs, but with a lower ceiling that had a number of the ugly green splotches. Tall windows from the stairwell area brought light into the hall from the back of the house, but there were no matching windows at the far end, just a solid doorway. The hall grew darker as we walked down it, toward the blasting music.

"You saw the ghost somewhere up here?" I asked Toolie, keeping my voice to a whisper since she hadn't told the whole family about it.

"The...crafts room," Toolie said. She pointed to the closed door at the very end of the corridor. The room beyond it would have been located directly above the foyer, at the front and center of the second floor looking out over the front garden. "Well, that's what it was supposed to be, a place for Gord to paint and me to do my sewing and make decorations, but...it never really took off."

"What do you mean?" I started toward the door, and Stacey walked with me. Toolie followed us slowly.

"Gord stays downstairs, mostly," she said. "And I...I don't know, I guess I never felt right in there."

We crossed an intersection with a smaller, narrower hallway, which ran from one side of the house to the other. Both ends of that cross-hall featured a window and a flight of steps down to the first floor. The loud music came from a door down the hall to our left, which was decorated with construction paper featuring a skull and crossbones and the words EVERYBODY STAY OUT! in angry red letters.

"Do you think the shadowy man I saw in the craft room is a poltergeist?" Toolie whispered.

"A male-energy poltergeist?" I asked. "That would be very rare. I'm not sure I've heard of one before, actually, but it's theoretically possible. Can we have a look?"

"Go ahead." Toolie trailed behind us as I approached the door. As I drew close to it, a feeling of dread began to fill me from the inside out, from the pit of my stomach to the tips of my shaking fingertips.

Calm down, Ellie, I told myself. *It's just a freaking sewing room.*

I looked at Stacey, and she nodded and swallowed. She felt something, too.

The handle was abnormally cold as I turned it and pushed the door open.

On the surface, the room beyond should have been fun and whimsical, and possibly the coolest room in the house. A row of windows looked out onto the front gardens and the street beyond, and a pair of tall, narrow glass doors led to the half-circle balcony out front. Floor-to-ceiling shelving and large cabinet doors were built into the other three walls.

Despite the copious amount of sunlight, shadows filled the room. I flipped the light switch, but nothing happened.

"Lights hardly ever work in there," Toolie said from where she stood, several feet behind us in the hall.

Boxes and furniture were stacked along the walls. A big Singer sewing machine sat on a work table, surrounded by dusty fabrics. Little plastic bags of buttons and beads, also coated in dust, occupied a pigeonhole rack next to the sewing machine. Everything looked abandoned.

The room was cold. I wished I'd brought my Mel-Meter to check the temperature and electromagnetic energy in the room. My instincts told me something dark and malevolent dwelled here.

"What exactly did you see?" I asked Toolie, who still remained in the hall, clearly not wanting to enter the room.

"A couple weeks ago, I was carrying a basket of laundry up to my bedroom." Toolie gestured at a door on the right side of the hall, which was the only door on that side, indicating that the master suite took up one quarter of the entire second floor. "When I came down the hall, I saw the door to the crafts room was open. That was strange, since it's always closed and none of us ever go in there.

"So I looked inside, thinking I might see Crane getting into some mischief. My little boy wasn't there. Somebody else was—or something else, I mean. It had the shape of a tall man, but it was all darkness, like it was made of smoke or shadows. No face, nothing, just darkness. He held something long and black in one hand. I can't say for sure what it was, but it was like some kind of leather strap. Little bits of metal glinted all over it.

"Well, I froze right there on the spot. I should have been running or screaming to see a strange man in my house, but I also knew it wasn't really a man, neither. I could feel him looking back at me, and I thought if I moved at all, he'd attack me like a startled snake. Or a hungry wolf. I can't explain why I didn't run, really, but the fear drained out all my go-juice."

"That sounds terrifying," I said, looking around the dark corners and the big cabinet doors. Some of those doors were big enough to conceal a person inside.

"After a minute—it couldn't have been much more than that, though it seemed to last hours, me and that thing staring at each other—he just up and vanished. Didn't move one way or another. He was gone so fast it made me wonder if it was all in my mind, and maybe I was going crazy. Then that door slammed itself shut!" Toolie pointed at the doorway between us. "That's when I could finally run. Just dropped the laundry basket and scooted off downstairs, but I didn't know how to explain it to anybody else. That was the last straw for me, though. I knew there was something bad in this house, something that meant to hurt us. That's when I got on the stick about finding some help, and I ended up getting in touch with y'all."

"Have you seen the dark figure again?" I asked.

"No, but I always get a bad feeling from that room now. Always kind of did, come to think of it, but of course it got worse after that."

I looked up at the ceiling. "I don't see any water stains here."

"Huh?" Toolie stepped closer to the doorway and looked up. "Yeah, I guess we haven't had any leaks in there. About the only room in the house where that's true."

"What else has your family experienced up here?" I asked.

"I've heard things in the attic a few times." Toolie backed up and pointed to one of the doors on her left, across from the single door to the master bedroom. Stacey and I joined her, closing the door behind us and trying not to look too eager to run out of the cold, creepy room.

"Bumping, a couple of footsteps...laughing, one time," Toolie continued. "High-pitched, like a woman or child. The worst was a few months ago, March or so. I was lying in my bed, and I heard a crash in the attic, and then a bunch of little bumps. It sounded like something was coming down the attic stairs. Then it got quiet. I don't believe I got back to sleep that night, but I didn't dare get up and try to see what was happening.

"The next morning, I came out here for a look." Toolie pulled open the door, revealing plain wooden steps ascending into darkness above. "There was Christmas ornaments all over the steps, red and green and some snowglobe ones we got at Wal-Mart a couple years ago. Something had picked up the box of decorations and threw them down the stairs. I knew it wasn't one of my kids, because I would have heard them walking up and down the hall. Even if they tried to tiptoe, I could hear it, cause the floorboards are so old and squeaky. Didn't nobody come down out of that attic all night."

"Did you look for any kind of animals up there?" I asked. "Squirrels, maybe?"

"I called out a pest removal man, but he didn't find nothing. No nest, no animal poop...Besides, what kind of animal laughs?"

"A hyena?" Stacey said.

"Well, there's no hyena up there!" Toolie said. "Not even a rat. We did find a lot of boxes overturned, and that was about it."

"Do you mind if we go up?" I asked.

"Suit yourself."

I reached for my flashlight, but it wasn't there. I hadn't loaded up my utility for this quick daytime walk-through of the house.

"How are the lights up there?" I asked Toolie.

"They work sometimes. Sometimes they cut off by themselves."

"We'll check it later. I'm more interested in speaking with your daughter right now."

Toolie took a deep breath. "We can try. Sometimes she don't want to talk much. Teenagers, I guess."

She led us back to the hallway intersection at the center of the second floor, then led us toward the door with the skull and the warning. The music thudded through the walls. The lyrics sounded something like *Massacre! Massacre! Yeah yeah yeah!* Deep stuff.

Too much stuff was happening at this house, and it made me feel overwhelmed and clueless. After what I'd felt in the disused crafts room, though, I was worried that at least one of the entities was malevolent. Friendly ghosts don't present themselves as shadow

figures.
> Toolie knocked on her daughter's door.

Chapter Three

Juniper's room was chaos, but not particularly unusual for a thirteen-year-old girl with rebellion on her mind. The heavy curtains were drawn across the windows, blotting out any sunlight. Posters hung on the walls, mostly bands of young boys with black clothes and pale skin. Laundry was everywhere.

The girl herself didn't look exactly like her pictures downstairs. Her hair was dyed an unnatural jet black, her eyeshadow and lip gloss were a dark purple that bordered on black, and the rest of her face was done up in stark white. A silver chalice pendant hung on her necklace, and she wore a long-sleeved black shirt and shredded jeans.

"What do you want?" Juniper snapped when she opened the door. Then she looked at us. "Who they hell are they?"

"Watch your language!" Toolie snapped, and the girl rolled her eyes. "This is Ellie and Stacey. They're professional ghost investigators."

"Ooh, they look really tough." Juniper scowled as she looked us over.

"Just tell them what's been going on in your room, Junie. Don't be rude."

"Right, because *now* you believe me," Juniper said. "Now that it's bugging you, suddenly you care about what happens to me."

"I always care about--" Toolie said.

"You thought I was lying!"

"Juniper," I said, "Can you just tell us what you've seen?"

The girl gave me a sullen look, then sighed.

"Like I've been telling Mom *forever*," Juniper said. "It moves stuff around in my room. Jewelry or whatever." She opened her door wider and pointed to a dresser jumbled with nail polish, mascaras, lipsticks, half-melted candles, and a stick-incense burner overflowing with ash. "It opens my drawers. Sometimes it does it quietly and I trip over them. Sometimes the whole drawer comes out and lands on the floor. Sometimes it rips down my posters, or my window curtains will move for no reason. Then there was the time my closet attacked me."

"What happened?" I looked at the open double doors to her closet, which was crammed full of clothes and shoes.

"I was just sitting here one night texting with Dayton. That's my *boyfriend*." She punctuated the word with a triumphant look at her mother, who shook her head and sighed. "My closet was shut tight. The doors flew open, and then everything started coming out, like flying through the air. The clothes landed wherever, but the hangers flew right at my head. I had to keep ducking while they banged into my headboard, and then I jumped on the floor. I was totally screaming. I mean, seriously, one of those things could've hooked me through the *eye* or something. Then I'd be *blind*."

"She was very scared," Toolie added.

"Yeah, and then Mom came in and *yelled* at me for making a big mess. She didn't believe me."

"I believe you now, honey."

"Yeah, so this house is haunted," Juniper said. She gave me an appraising look. "Can you really do something about it?"

"That's our job," I told her. "Has it ever hurt you?"

"No, but it totally could."

I glanced up at Juniper's ceiling. There were four green splotches scattered across it.

"Has your ceiling leaked?" I asked her.

"Yes! And it's so gross! It smells like puked-up piss," Juniper said.

"Watch your language!" Toolie snapped.

"Tell me more about the time your closet erupted," I said. "Was anything else happening that day? Something that might have upset you?"

"I was fighting with Dayton," she said. "But it was all his fault. He was totally flirting with my friend China, like right in front of everyone at this party."

"What party?" Toolie asked.

"It's none of your business!" Juniper snapped.

As she shouted, a few paperbacks tumbled off her shelf and thudded to the floor. They looked like vampire-romance novels.

We all jumped and looked over at the fallen books.

"See?" Juniper said. "All the time."

"Mom, who are those ladies?" a new voice asked. A boy with dark, rusty hair like Gordon stood in the hallway, wearing a Captain America t-shirt. Crane still looked like his pictures downstairs—he hadn't reached the corruption of his teenage years yet. The seven-year-old had stepped outside of his room, which was decorated with Marvel superheroes and a few space rockets.

"They're here to help with the strange things around the house," Toolie said.

"You mean the ghosts," Crane said.

"It's nice to meet you, Crane!" Stacey said.

Crane studied Stacey, then me, his green eyes very bright, as if trying to take in every detail of us. Then he turned to his mom.

"Luke and Noah don't like them," Crane told her.

"Who are Luke and Noah?" I asked.

"Just his imaginary friends," Toolie told me. "They don't seem to like much of anything that goes on around here."

"Can you tell me what they look like?" I asked.

Crane shook his head.

"How old are they?" I asked.

"They don't want me to tell you about them," Crane said.

"Why not?"

Crane looked at me again, then backed into his room and closed the door.

"He's going through a difficult phase, too," Toolie said.

"You mean a dorky-weirdo-freak phase," Juniper said.

"You're one to talk!" Toolie snapped.

"Whatever." Juniper rolled her eyes again. "Can you two get rid of the ghosts or not?"

"I think we can," I said.

"Then please do it," she said. "And leave me alone. I have, like, homework to do or something." She turned to look at the video game paused on her television as she closed the door.

"Those kids." Toolie shook her head. "You wonder how things got like this, with everybody fighting about everything. We all used to get along so good."

"The energy in a haunted house can be negative," I said. "Anger, depression, and anxiety are common. We'll do what we can to lift that dark cloud."

"I hope you can."

We returned to the back patio on the first floor to rejoin Gord.

"How did it...go?" he asked.

"I think I talked their ears off," Toolie replied, sinking into a wooden deck recliner next to him.

"You have a lot of activity here," I told them. Stacey and I dropped into lawn chairs. "I think there's a good chance of a multiple haunting, with complications. We have an entity obsessed with water, creating problems inside and outside the house." I glanced at the stagnant unwanted pool at the center of their back yard. "We have something that seems attracted to games and toys. I'm guessing that may be the entity in the attic, the one that laughs and threw the Christmas decorations down the stairs."

"Is it a...kid's ghost?" Gord asked.

"It could be," I said. "You may have something dark and disturbing in the craft room upstairs, too."

"I always got a...bad feeling there," Gord said.

"We could be talking about at least three separate entities, based on the different behavior patterns," I said. "On top of that, there's a good chance you have a poltergeist." I quickly reviewed what Toolie and Juniper had told us, including the books that had jumped off Juniper's shelves while we spoke with her.

"Good Lord," Toolie said. "We knew it was bad, but...that's four ghosts?"

"What do we do?" Gord asked.

"I want to approach this in three different ways," I said. "First, Stacey and I will need to set up our cameras and microphones for an overnight observation so we can get a better look at the entities causing the problems. In my experience, that might take a few nights to get more complete results. In the meantime, I want to bring in a psychic medium for a walk-through, just to get some extra impressions and a clearer idea of what we're dealing with here." *Because there's way too much going on for me to sort it all out,* I thought. I prefer the hard numerical data gathered by my instruments to the vague, sometimes misleading information provided by psychics, but you gotta do what you gotta do.

Stacey naturally grinned at the news that we would be calling Jacob.

"We'll research the history of the house to see if we can put some names and faces with these unwanted inhabitants," I said. "Is there anything you can tell us? Any reason the house might be haunted? Murders, suicides, and other strange deaths are usually involved, or at least a great deal of misery and suffering."

"We don't know much about the house's past," Toolie said. "My cousin might know things. I've asked her before, but she said she never lived here, just inherited the place from her aunt. But I felt like she was holding something back."

"Like she didn't want to admit that she'd invited you to live in a haunted house," I said.

"Exactly!" Toolie nodded. "Now that you put it that way, that might just be it. Or maybe she just don't really know anything about it."

"I'd like to speak with her if I can."

"I don't think that's a good idea," Toolie said. "She insists she's never seen a ghost here. Thinks I'm going crazy."

"There's one other step I'd like to take, if it's okay with the two of you," I said. "I'd really like to do some ESP testing with Juniper. It could help us determine whether she may have latent psychic abilities that would enable her to create a poltergeist."

Stacey's eyebrows raised—this was new to her.

Toolie and Gord traded puzzled looks.

"It's perfectly safe," I said. "My boss, Calvin Eckhart, would administer it, since he has more experience with that. If Juniper shows no signs of those abilities, then it's much less likely we're dealing with a poltergeist."

"And what if she did make that poltergeist? Then what?" Toolie asked.

"Then we teach her to stop feeding it," I said. "A poltergeist, once it's active, is a spiritual parasite. It will keep draining energy from its creator, making itself more powerful and its creator weaker and weaker."

"Oh, goodness! That's awful!" Toolie said.

"Do...whatever you think will help," Gord said. "We need some peace...around here."

I nodded. "We'll get started right away. Tomorrow's Friday—is that a good night for us to set up our gear?"

"Any night's fine," Toolie said. "Sooner begun, sooner done."

"How long...will it take...to get rid of them?" Gord asked.

"We'll work as quickly as we can, Mr. Paulding," I said. "When we understand more about your haunting, we can put together our eradication plan."

He smiled a little, as if he liked the sound of *eradication plan*. "Thank you," he said. "I just want my...family to be safe."

"So do we," I said. "We're here to make this house safe for all of you."

As we walked away from the house, through the patchy front garden, Stacey said, "Lots of crazy stuff happening there."

"It's an old house," I said. "I think we might have layers of hauntings built up over the years. That could get messy."

"Do you think the ghosts are dangerous?" she asked, while we climbed into the van.

"The poltergeist sounds like the most dangerous one." I started up the engine.

"How do we remove poltergeists? Does a normal ghost trap work?"

"It can be easier than that, or much more difficult," I said. "It really depends on how cooperative the poltergeist's creator is."

"Juniper doesn't seem too cooperative about anything," Stacey said. "What about the shadow man in that crafts room upstairs?"

"He worries me," I said. "That room felt dark and cold to me. And...malevolent."

"Me, too," Stacey said.

"We need to figure out who he is. Then we'll know how to kick him out. Or trap him."

I drove through the city as the night crept in, bringing darkness to the old mansions and the tree-shrouded streets. Savannah is a city of graveyards, including countless graves, even ancient Indian burial grounds, that have been paved over to make room for new streets and buildings over the years. The whole city is really a cemetery, and the dead are everywhere, haunting the gardens and marble colonnades of the Historic District. I really love it here.

Chapter Four

The next morning was all about research. Stacey and I headed down to the Bull Street Library, a lovely marble-columned temple of knowledge with a large collection of local history and genealogy documents. Our clients' home had been built in 1841, so we had to search through almost two centuries of deed transfers and obituaries related to their address, trying to find the sort of tragedies and deaths that can lead to hauntings. Some of this data has been digitized, some is on microfilm, and some is only available as crumbling yellow paperwork.

It was going to be a long day of digging through old information, but Stacey found a way to make it even longer.

"So...do we call Jacob today?" Stacey asked, while we sat at the big microfilm machines looking at old newspapers.

"Not yet. I want some hard facts before I start trying to interpret any psychic impressions."

"But we could let him know we're going to need him, right? Maybe tomorrow or Sunday?"

"Go ahead and call him," I said, mainly to prevent her from going on and on about Jacob and how fascinating his psychic abilities were. "Just remember that dating a psychic can get complicated."

"Who's dating?" Stacey's brow furrowed. "Complicated how?"

"Do you want a boyfriend who can read your mind?"

"Uh...can he do that?" Now she looked worried. "I thought he only communicated with dead people."

"Who knows? Maybe he's listening to your thoughts right now." I gave her a somewhat evil grin.

"Seriously?" Stacey glanced around the quiet library room, as if expecting to see Jacob there. "Have *you* ever dated a psychic? Not that I'm dating Jacob or anything."

"Nope." I scrolled through more obituaries from the 1850's.

"Are you dating anyone now?" Stacey asked, giving me a little smile. "You don't talk about yourself very much."

"Probably because there's not much to say. I work, I read books, I have a cat."

"No boyfriend or anything?"

"I think that's pretty obvious from my last statement."

"I know plenty of cute college guys if you want one," Stacey said.

"I'm twenty-six, Stacey. They're probably a little young for me."

"Young, handsome, energetic..."

"Immature, obnoxious..." I countered. "Come on, most guys *my* age are immature."

"So what kind of guy are you looking for?" Stacey asked.

"Right now? I'm looking for one who died tragically in our clients' house and might be haunting it to this day."

"Pfft, all business."

"Exactly," I said. I didn't feel like reviewing my fairly empty romantic history with Stacey right then. I just don't like to get too close to too many people. Saying that out loud would run a dangerous risk of talking about Anton Clay, the antebellum pyromaniac ghost who had burned down my house and killed my parents. No, thank you.

I managed to steer our attention back to the work at hand. Stacey was actually quiet for a full twenty minutes before she said, quite a bit too loudly for the library: "Holy cow!"

"What is it?" I whispered my words, by way of reminding her to keep her voice down.

"Read this," Stacey said in a not-so-quiet stage whisper. She pointed to a blurry article on the screen before her, printed in the less-than-pleasant blocky font of newspapers from the mid-1800's.

This one was dated January 1853. The headline was:
MOTHER, CHILDREN LOST IN DROWNING ACCIDENT.

"Catherine Ridley, thirty-six, died on Tuesday after drowning in the pond behind her house. Also deceased are her sons Noah, 12, and Luke, 10, and daughter Eliza, 8," Stacey read aloud.

"Noah and Luke?" I leaned over for a closer look. Those were the names of the invisible friends mentioned by Crane, our client's seven-year-old son.

"Exactly. And this is just crazy. What are the odds of four people drowning in a pond at once? You'd think they'd suspect murder," Stacey said.

"And this," I said, and I read aloud: "'Catherine's husband, Isaiah, died tragically on December 26.' We'd better find that obit. And any subsequent reports about these deaths."

We searched forward and backward in time. Stacey quickly found the death notice for Isaiah Ridley, who "died unexpectedly and tragically at his home" the day after Christmas. He was described as a prominent attorney who'd been very involved in public life.

"What the duck?" Stacey asked, having been trained by her mother to avoid actual swearing. "What does that mean, unexpectedly and tragically?"

"It means the newspaper wanted to be discreet and was worried about damage to the family or their reputation," I said. "Something happened they didn't want to put into print."

"Stupid tactful newspaper editors!" Stacey said.

"Let's see what else we can find."

Despite the strange, vague manner in which the newspaper initially described the family's deaths, there were no follow-up articles to shed more light on what had happened. The closest we could find was a notice, two months after the wife and kids died, that the house had been put up for auction to pay debts and back taxes. The Ridley family must have had some financial trouble towards the end.

We kept digging, but found nothing else about their deaths, though we found other articles that mentioned Isaiah Ridley in connection with assorted legal actions by cotton and shipping concerns. He was also mentioned as a city council member at one point, as well as an investor in the Georgia Canal and Railroad Company, which quietly failed about a year before Isaiah's death.

The genealogy librarian helped us find the family's death

certificates. Fortunately, they had been digitized, so there wasn't a lot of digging around in old boxes and sneezing out dust. The librarian printed out paper copies for us, and we returned to our table to study them.

For Catherine Ridley and her three children, the cause of death was listed as "asphyxiation." No huge surprise there, if they'd drowned in a pond. There was no additional information, though, no hint of why all four people had died at once.

Isaiah's death certificate offered a new tidbit of information. His cause of death was given as "gunshot."

"What?" Stacey asked. "If he was murdered, the papers would have said something about it, right?"

"Right. But the newspaper chose to be discreet instead...so I'm guessing it was suicide," I said.

"Oh, that could make sense. So maybe he loses all his money on this bankrupt railroad company, then he shoots himself on the day after Christmas." Stacey shook her head. "That's always kind of a depressing day, anyway, am I right?"

"It all fits, but the real mystery is the wife and kids."

"Do you think..." Stacey glanced around the library, which had few patrons at the moment, then lowered her voice to a whisper. "Do you think his ghost killed them? Like drowned them in the pond somehow?"

"I wouldn't jump to any conclusions," I said. "People who commit suicide are turning their violence inward, not lashing out at other people. Why would he want to return from the grave and murder his entire family?"

"Maybe he was crazed," Stacey said. "Maybe it was like one of those murder-suicide cases, only he got the order wrong."

"Maybe," I said. Stacey's theory didn't sound very compelling to me, but I understood that she was just trying to glue together the random pieces of data we'd uncovered so far.

"Then what do you think happened?" she asked.

"I don't have any idea. We're going to have to dig a little deeper."

Stacey sighed. The historical research clearly bored her—she was much more about finding the ghosts in person and capturing their images and sounds. Long hours at the library made her fidgety.

"Let's stop for lunch," I suggested.

"Great idea!" Stacey leaped to her feet so fast the chair toppled back behind her. As she picked it up, she said, "Can we go to

Butterhead Greens Cafe? It's right down the block and they have this great quinoa salad."

"I've been there. I'm not that into quinoa, though."

I dropped our little stack of printouts and photocopies into a folder as we walked toward the exit. It was a miserably thin stack, without much evidence for our case.

As we strolled up the sidewalk, shaded from the pounding summer sun by ancient oaks dripping with Spanish moss, I took out my cell phone and called Grant Patterson, one of my boss's old friends and a fellow at the Savannah Historical Association. Grant is a semi-if-not-mostly retired attorney, though he's only fifty-two, with a passion for history and finely tailored suits. He's the confirmed bachelor scion of an old banking and shipping family. His specialty is sordid gossip from our city's long and sometimes dark history, which makes him valuable when we're investigating old murders and mysterious deaths.

"Tell me the restless undead are marching up River Street," he said when he answered the phone. "We could all use a little excitement."

"Nothing that big, unfortunately," I said. "Can you check up something in the Historical Association archives for me?"

"I hope you don't mean today," Grant replied. "It's nearly the cocktail hour."

"I've got two p.m."

"Precisely. What long-forgotten horror will we be exploring this time?"

"The Ridley family," I said. "Five of them died within two weeks of each other. Two parents, three children. Ever heard of them?"

"I have not. How did they die?"

"The father, Isaiah, died of a gunshot the day after Christmas. The papers didn't report the manner of death, and they didn't call it a murder."

"Suicide," Grant murmured.

"That's what we're thinking. Apparently the mom and kids all drowned together in a pond on the property not long after that."

"How strange. Were *they* murdered?"

"That's what we need you to figure out," I said. "It doesn't make any sense to me, and it was like the newspaper didn't want to publicize the details. It sounds like Isaiah was kind of prominent in town, so maybe they were trying to protect his family's reputation."

"This sounds scandalous," Grant said. "How interesting. Let's have the details, dear, and I'll see what I can turn up for you."

I gave him the address of our clients' home and all the names of the family members and the dates of their deaths—everything we'd found so far.

"Any idea of when you can have something for us?" I asked.

"So impatient! I'll have what I have when I have it, and not a moment before."

"Tomorrow?" I suggested.

"Working on a Saturday violates my most treasured values and beliefs," Grant replied, "But I may make an exception for you, Ellie."

"Thank you, Grant."

By this point, Stacey and I had reached the cafe, which occupied the first floor of an old house on Bull Street. The cafe was painted an eye-catching solid black with screaming green trim at the windows and doors, which made it stand out in a neighborhood defined by the massive brick Savannah College of Art and Design building across the street, two blocks wide and surrounded by old trees. The customers were largely students—at twenty-six, I felt a little old for the crowd, but Stacey was four years younger and fit right in.

I ate a big, fancy salad with blue cheese, avocado, and almonds, while Stacey had her quinoa and again offered to try and spice up my love life, nodding at a cute college boy eating a grilled chicken sandwich at another table, a boy she claimed to know. I considered it—the guy *was* cute—but I declined Stacey's offer. For the moment, anyway.

Then we each went home to rest so we could stay up all night. It was time to see the ghosts for ourselves.

Chapter Five

We returned to the Paulding home on Friday evening, about an hour before sunset. Stacey and I had only had time for quick naps at our respective apartments, so we picked up some potent, espresso-laced coffee from Goose Feathers Cafe.

A big downside to this job is the hours—you spend a lot of time at libraries and archives, which are open during the day and close early, and a lot of time doing overnight observations at haunted houses. Sometimes I'll find myself awake for twenty-four or forty-eight hours at a clip, especially when there's a dangerous ghost involved and I'm worried about my clients. So coffee is pretty critical to my existence.

Stacey and I sat with Gord and Toolie in the first-floor living room that was cluttered and overfurnished with its accumulation of antique divans, settees, and other fancy sorts of sofas and chairs. The late-in-the-day sunlight through the tall back windows painted everyone a bloody shade of orange, like a gentle omen of death for us all. The two kids were upstairs, presumably occupied with their tablets, phones, and televisions.

Toolie had set out cups of iced tea and a plate of some really great chocolate chip cookies for us. There's no greater hospitality than offering your guests chocolate.

"We found a number of deaths over the years," I told them, catching them up on our research. "You expect that with a house this old. One family in particular interested me." I quickly filled them in on Isaiah Ridley's probable suicide and the as-yet-unexplained deaths of his wife and three children two weeks later.

Not surprisingly, they had a visible reaction when I told them the names of Ridley's two boys, Noah and Luke. Toolie flinched in her overstuffed brocaded armchair, while Gord's eyes widened and he gasped noisily through his oxygen tubes.

"Crane's invisible friends," Toolie whispered.

"The boys' ages were twelve and ten when they died," I said. "Does that match Crane's friends?"

"He does say they're...older boys," Gord said.

"Did he have those invisible friends prior to moving here?" I asked.

"No," Toolie said, and Gord shook his head. "They showed up right after Crane's sixth birthday. We'd just moved here, and we didn't know any kids to invite for him, so it was just his parents and his sister for his little party. Kind of sad. We figured he made up his invisible friends because of that."

"But you think...they're real," Gord said.

"That's the reason we're looking at the Ridley family in particular," I said. "That, and the drownings. Ghosts are obsessed with their own deaths. Your constant water problems could be related to that." I glanced up at the green stains on the living room ceiling.

"So we have two ghosts," Toolie said.

"At least two," I said. "We should have much more information after tonight, but there's still the possibility of a poltergeist with your daughter, Juniper. Young people tend to create them in times of high stress, and when the house is already haunted, the psychically charged atmosphere makes it easier for them to generate a poltergeist. It's all unconscious and unintentional, of course. The young person has no idea that she's created it and is continuing to feed it. Did you speak to her about the ESP tests?"

"Yes..." Toolie said, but her tone didn't exactly fill me with hope.

"What did she say?" I asked, after it was apparent Toolie wasn't going to continue on her own.

"She didn't seem to like the idea," Toolie said. "She says 'no' to just about anything I ask her to do these days, though. She wasn't always like that. Even a year ago, she was still a sweet little..." Toolie shook her head.

"Maybe I can speak with her, Mrs. Paulding," Stacey said. "I'm good with kids, and I'm not that much older than Juniper."

"Yeah, you guys can talk boy bands together," I said, and Stacey gave me a subtle annoyed look, narrowing her eyes just slightly.

"You may as well try, but she's stubborn as a mule in quicksand, like my daddy used to say." Toolie snorted. "He was usually saying it about Momma. Maybe Juniper inherited that."

"We'll speak to her," I said. "There are a couple of other interesting deaths. A woman drowned in an upstairs bathtub in 1915. Her name was Mathilda Knowles. I gather the Knowles family eventually sold it to your cousin's folks, Mrs. Paulding. She wasn't that old, only about forty-five and in good health, as far as we could tell. Since there's the connection with water again, we're going to look more closely at her, but I think the Ridley family ghosts are probably the main issue here."

"This certainly is interesting," Toolie said. "Do you think the boys are the ones messing around with the games and the TV?"

"It's possible. We'll set up cameras in here tonight." I gestured toward the antique cupboard housing the board games. "Maybe we'll pull some items out to try and draw their attention. We'll need cameras in several places, upstairs and down...if y'all don't mind, we should probably get started with our set-up. Unless you have other questions?"

Gord and Toolie looked at each other.

"I'm sure we have a thousand," Toolie said. "But I wouldn't know where to start, so go on and do what you need to do."

"Thank you, Mr. and Mrs. Paulding," I said, and Gord gave us a worried frown as we stood up and walked out toward the van.

We started downstairs, positioning thermal and night vision video cameras in the living room so we could see the game cupboard and the phonograph. Stacey set up a high-sensitivity microphone in the middle of the room, on a rosewood end table crammed between two hefty old chairs with wide wings and high backs.

We stuck a thermal camera in the downstairs powder room to watch the sink, which frequently turned itself on at night. Most of the reported activity was upstairs, though, so we concentrated our gear up there.

Thermal and night vision cameras went into the cold,

unpleasant-feeling crafts room at the front of the second story, where Toolie had seen the dark apparition. My skin crawled in that room, and I thought about how she'd described it—the tall male figure staring at her, silent and unmoving, and then the door suddenly slamming itself closed.

The crafts room was full of cardboard boxes as well as the dusty sewing machine and its forgotten shelves of beads and cloth. I opened a few cabinet doors, which were as big as regular doors between rooms, and found most of them crammed full of assorted junk, too. I didn't know how the family could stand living in a house so cluttered, but I supposed it wasn't their stuff in the first place, so they weren't free to throw anything out.

I tried the doors to the front balcony, but they didn't budge. It was strange how a room could have so many big windows yet remain so dim. That's a haunted house for you.

Stacey and I were happy to get out of that room as quickly as possible.

We placed another night vision camera in the hall, angled to watch the sink in one of the bathrooms.

"What's next?" Stacey glanced down the intersecting hall at the closed door to Juniper's room, from which more harsh, angry music leaked out. Our options were to go talk to the moody teenage girl or go set up in the creepy attic where Toolie had heard strange thumps, crashes, and footsteps.

"The attic," I said. "It sounds easier than talking to the girl."

The door to the attic steps creaked as we opened it. I felt around the dim wall until I found the light switch, then I flipped it.

Nothing happened for a moment. Then there was a crackling sound, and a little weak yellow light glowed overhead. I turned on my high-powered tactical flashlight to ward off any curious ghosts. A concentrated three-thousand-lumen beam will send pesky spirits back into the shadows, but it doesn't hurt them, and it certainly doesn't help you capture them. Still, you should never go into a haunted old attic without one.

I led the way up the stairs, built in the uncomfortably steep and narrow fashion of the olden days. It was better than climbing a ladder, though. It's hard to run for your life down a ladder.

The attic was gloomy and spacious, a musty wooden cavern full of dust and spiderwebs. Three bare bulbs spaced along the ceiling gave a little light, but one was buzzing and flickering, like it would burn out at any moment or explode and rain glass and sparks on our heads, if we were really lucky.

Heavy timbers crisscrossed the attic at steep angles, many of them conveniently positioned right at head-bashing height. Stacey and I had to duck under them as we explored the attic. First we passed through a couple of holiday areas, including a big plastic tree with a string of lights still tangled in it, next to a grinning, life-size stuffed Santa Claus with his mitten raised in greeting. One of Santa's glass eyes was missing, giving him a freakish pirate look. Our flashlights found Easter baskets still packed with plastic green grass, then a box overflowing with Halloween masks and plastic kid's costumes.

Ghosts like attics and basements for several reasons. For one thing, those areas are usually left dark, quiet, and deserted most of the time, so they can obsess over their issues undisturbed.

Another reason, though, is that the attic, the basement, the storage crawlspace, sometimes the garage, are like the house's subconscious. We store away the seasonal items, and we store all the things we don't really need but can't throw away because we feel too attached to them. Ghosts are drawn to those accumulated geological layers of memory and meaning. They're emotional beings more than rational ones.

"See anything?" Stacey whispered. We'd reached an area of deeper storage, with dust-coated antique furniture, a grandfather clock with a broken face, and wooden crates full of who-knows-what. Old wooden pull toys and puppets were heaped in one corner, along with a rickety rocking horse and a tricycle with a rusty seat promising tetanus to any child who sat upon it.

"Just a couple centuries' worth of junk," I said. "This attic is an ideal ghost habitat, lots of hiding places, lots of old stuff that had emotional significance to somebody."

"Where should we set up the cameras?"

I considered it. The room was enormous, running the full width and length of the house below, all the walls still deep in shadow even when the dinky overhead light bulbs were lit.

"Point them in different directions, try to cover as much area as you can," I told Stacey. "Definitely get the stairs in the shot. We might catch something coming or going."

Stacey began setting up the tripods. I let her handle the work, since she has a bachelor's in film, and her job title is tech manager.

My job title is lead investigator, so it was my job to stand around and lead, I guess.

I closed my eyes, trying to get a sense of the room. It was unsettling, but not cold and scary like the craft room. There might have been something there. I don't go by feelings, though, so I brought out my Mel Meter, a device that measures both temperature and electromagnetic energy.

While Stacey prepared and tested the cameras, I did another slow lap around the attic, ducking under timbers and weaving through furniture. The EMF readings spiked a few times for no obvious reason—no electrical outlets or anything like that. They were strong, five to six milligaus, indicating an active presence.

The attic wasn't particularly cold, but it wasn't as roasting hot as it should have been, considering it was July in Georgia. It was actually a pretty pleasant temperature, like the presence was just there to help cool the house.

"Are you feeling anything weird up here?" Stacey asked when I returned. She'd finished the cameras.

"I got a few energy spikes," I said. "The temperature is lower than you'd expect."

"But it doesn't feel creepy," she said. "I felt like something was watching me, but it was almost benign, like a house pet. I didn't see anything."

"If there's anything up here, the worst it's done is throw a box of Christmas ornaments down the steps," I said.

"I thought that was the poltergeist," Stacey said.

"Or it might have been the poltergeist. There's too much going on here. Come on, let's get moving. Maybe you can dazzle Juniper with your charm and personality. I really want her to do those psychic tests with Calvin."

Chapter Six

Stacey knocked on the door with the skull and bones warning us away. There was no answer, so she knocked a little louder.

"What?" screamed an angry banshee voice. The door flung open, and Juniper stood there scowling, ready to snap. Then she saw her mother wasn't present, and she relaxed a little. "Oh. Yeah. You're the vampire slayers or whatever."

"That's us," I said, my voice barely audible over the blasting music behind her. "We just wanted to ask you about--"

"Go away!" Juniper screamed, and I recoiled, a little startled.

She was looking past me. Her little brother Crane had silently opened the door behind us and leaned out to watch.

"But I want to know what you're doing!" Crane shouted back.

"Leave us alone!" she shouted.

"Hey, buddy, we can talk later if you like." Stacey patted Crane's shoulder. "We're just going to talk about boring girl stuff with your sister."

"You're gonna talk about the ghosts," Crane replied with a pout. Well, the kid was right.

"Stop being such a buttbone!" Juniper said, and he stuck out his tongue at her. She sighed and turned to me. "You want to talk in my room? He's being a total nozzle today."

"What's a nozzle?" Crane asked.

"You are," Juniper informed him.

"Yeah, let's check out your room, Juniper!" Stacey said, nudging her way inside.

Crane continued staring at us until Juniper closed the door behind her.

"Sorry, that's so embarrassing." Juniper sat on the bed and gestured to a small armchair strewn with dirty laundry and old candy wrappers.

"Go ahead, Stacey." I gestured for her to sit on the laundry chair, suppressing a grin. Stacey, trapped by a sense of manners and hospitality, reluctantly took her seat, perching herself on the front edge of the cushion.

"Can you turn that music down a little? It's kind of hard to talk," Stacey said. That was Stacey, relating to Juniper and connecting to her on her own level.

Juniper gave an overblown sigh, grabbed a thin black wafer of a remote, and turned down the stereo.

"What's going on?" Juniper asked, dropping to sit on her bed again. "Did you find any ghosts yet?"

"We'll be watching for them all night," Stacey said. "Do they freak you out?"

"I guess." Juniper shrugged. "Stuff's always bugging me. If it's not the ghost, it's my brother--"

Her stereo turned itself up to ear-punching maximum volume, rattling the room with the screeching voice of an angst-filled boy-band singer. Juniper shouted and pointed the remote at her small, sleek stereo, but the volume didn't drop. She shook her head and crossed the room to turn it off manually. When that didn't work, she yanked the plug from the wall, and the stereo finally fell silent.

"You see what I mean?" She dropped the stereo plug to the floor like a comedian ending her act. "This is my life."

"Juniper, do you know what a poltergeist is?" Stacey asked.

"Yeah. My parents told me you think I have one. But I already knew what they were. Do you think I made the poltergeist? You think it's all my fault?" Juniper looked at me, as if she didn't quite trust Stacey as an authority on the subject. It's the glasses, I think. They sometimes make people think I'm smarter than I am.

"I don't think it's your fault," I said. "Nobody creates a poltergeist on purpose. Why would you? They hang around harassing you, breaking your stuff, feeding on your energy. Who would want that?"

"I don't know." She shrugged and looked at the floor. Her voice dropped to a whisper. "It just feels like I did it."

"Why do you say that?" I asked.

She shrugged. "How can I stop it?"

"First, we're not even sure it's definitely a poltergeist," I said. "Maybe we'll learn more tonight. One way you can help us would be to take a test to evaluate any latent psychic powers you might have."

"My parents told me. What kind of tests?"

"Just some standard things—Zener cards, hidden objects, maybe a PK test."

"Is that like with needles?" Juniper asked. "Like taking blood?"

"Huh? No," I said. "It tests whether you can move objects with your mind."

"Weird. I don't know." She shrugged.

I approached her bookshelf, where I'd noticed a few volumes about Wicca and Tarot cards tucked among the vampire romances and horror comics. Some of them were books I'd read as a teenager, Llewellyn Press books on spell-casting and divination, and some of them were darker, their black covers adorned with lurid pentagrams. It looked like Juniper was going through the same kind of phase. I think it's perfectly natural to be obsessed with the occult for a while after you see a nineteenth-century ghost burn down your house and murder your parents—or anytime you have ghosts infesting in your house, I suppose. Juniper was trying to cope with restless spirits and a troublesome poltergeist.

"This was one of my favorites as a kid," I said, pulling out a book called *Earth Magic and Your Kitchen*. "I tried to cast a spell on my algebra teacher."

"Did it work?" Juniper asked, leaning toward me with sudden interest.

"I don't know. I wanted him to stop picking on me in class. He ended up having a heart attack. He didn't die, but he was gone the rest of the year. I stopped messing with it after that. Do you ever try to do the things in these books, Juniper? Or do you just read them?"

"Just read," she said quickly. "I mean, who's going to sit around and do that stuff with me?" Juniper looked between Stacey and me.

"How do you get to be a ghost hunter, anyway?"

"You have to go to college," I told her, since I figured her parents wouldn't mind that answer. "So, what do you say? Will you do the test?"

"Can I help with your ghost hunting stuff, too?" she asked.

"Definitely!" Stacey said, hopping to her feet. "We'd like to set up some gear to monitor your room. Can you help us carry it from the van?" Clever Stacey, roping the girl into doing some free labor.

"What kind of stuff?" Juniper asked her.

"Special cameras and microphones to help us find the ghosts."

"Oh, yeah." Juniper slid off her bed. "Whatever I can do."

"Does that mean you'll do the tests, too?" I asked.

"If they say I'm psychic, does that mean I made the poltergeist?" she asked.

"It means it's possible," I said. "But you have to understand it's not your fault, either way."

Juniper nodded.

A few minutes later, her mother looked surprised to see the girl carrying equipment in with us.

"You aren't getting in the way, are you?" Toolie asked.

"No, Mom, I'm not."

"She's a big help, ma'am," Stacey said, flashing a smile. Toolie just gave us a worried look, like she didn't want her daughter to get too chummy with the weirdo ghost investigators. She frowned as we went upstairs together. I wondered if she was thinking about her daughter's apparent interest in witchcraft.

We set up a pair of video cameras and a microphone in Juniper's room. I doubted we would get anything on the microphone—poltergeists are creatures of action, not words—but I didn't stop Stacey from setting it up, since Juniper seemed so interested in our process.

"Have y'all ever really seen a ghost on these things?" Juniper asked.

"Yes, ma'am," Stacey said. "Sometimes they're just cold spots or little orbs, but sometimes you get an image so clear it makes you jump out of your socks."

"Would tomorrow afternoon work for the testing?" I asked Juniper.

"Whatever, I'm not busy," she said, looking between the cameras. "Should I try to make the poltergeist do something?"

"Are you able to do that?" I asked, surprised by the idea.

"Uh, I don't know. Can I? I mean, it's my poltergeist. It should listen to me."

"They typically don't," I said. "But...honestly, trying won't hurt anything." I couldn't say whether I was humoring the girl or genuinely curious whether it might work.

"Okay. Um..." Juniper stood at the foot of the bed, took a deep breath, and pointed at her laundry chair. "Poltergeist...attack!"

All three of us watched the chair. Not a single dirty sock or spiky black belt stirred.

"Maybe I need a better target." Juniper grabbed a stuffed animal from the floor and tossed it into the chair. It looked like a zombie rabbit, about two feet high, bright green, with yellow button eyes and lots of visible Frankenstein's-monster stitching.

"Hey, that's pretty cool," Stacey said. "A zombie bunny."

"There's a bunch of different Zombie Zoo animals," Juniper said. "I really want the kangaroo. It has a zipper pouch with a zombie joey inside. So ugly and cute." She balled her fists on her hips and stared at the stuffed rabbit, her jaw clenched.

I couldn't help sharing an amused smile with Stacey. The girl was dedicated.

"Okay, poltergeist!" Juniper stabbed all ten fingers in the air toward the zombie bunny as if trying to cast a spell. "Go, poltergeist! Sic him!"

Stacey and I couldn't help bursting into laughter at the words "Sic him!" and, after a second, Juniper laughed with us.

"What on Earth is happening in here?" Toolie walked into the room, frowning even more as she looked at the three of us laughing at the apparently hilarious stuffed bunny rabbit.

"I was trying to get my poltergeist to attack," Juniper said.

"Oh, my word." Toolie gave me a questioning look.

"Don't worry, Mom, it didn't do anything," Juniper rushed to say. "Maybe I just need to tell it to bug me, and it'll leave me alone."

"I think it's getting to be bedtime, Juniper," Toolie said, but she was still looking at me.

"Nine o' clock? On a Friday?" Juniper asked.

"We'll get out of the way," I said. "Juniper, if you could do us a big favor, just go about your night as you normally would."

"Okay." Juniper nodded as we left.

"Listen," Toolie said in the hall, after closing her daughter's door.

"We've had some trouble with her getting into, well, black magic and occult nonsense. We do not want to encourage her. I hope you understand."

"I'm sorry, Mrs. Paulding," I said. "We're only trying to understand the problem. What kind of trouble did you have?"

"We found her up here with a friend one night," Toolie said. "They were doing *Tarot* cards. By *candlelight*." She shook her head. "It was troubling."

"We'll be sure to avoid anything like that," I said as we walked toward the stairs. "The psychic tests we're doing tomorrow were developed by parapsychology departments at major universities." I didn't mention that most of said parapsychology departments had since been closed down.

"So she agreed to do them? And she offered to help you with your work?" Toolie shook her head. "Miracles, miracles."

Downstairs, we prepared the living room in a way we hoped might draw the ghost's attention. Stacey and I set out a game of *Monopoly* for four players, and we arranged the *Candy Land* game with the little plastic children at random points on the board, as if a game were already in play.

At the phonograph machine, we carefully slipped a record of a song called "Cheyenne" by somebody named Billy Murray out of its stiff yellow sleeve. We placed it on the turntable in case the ghost felt like cranking it up again.

I walked with Stacey to our van outside, which is our mobile nerve center for all the cameras, microphones, motion detectors, and other gear we spread throughout the haunted houses we investigate. The rear of the cargo van has a couple of narrow, extremely uncomfortable drop-down bunks, plus racks and bins to hold our equipment. An array of small, built-in monitors enables our tech manager—that's Stacey—to sit and watch activity all over the house at once.

As the lead investigator, I would go back inside and watch for ghosts in person. Sometimes they don't show up on camera, but are very clear to living eyes.

"All ready?" Stacey asked me while we strapped on the little headsets that would keep us in voice contact all night. I don't really like wearing the headsets, because they remind me of some nightmarish orthodontic gear I wore as a teenager.

"Yep," I said. "I'm not too worried about this house yet. As long as Mr. Creep stays upstairs in the crafts room."

"Yeah, that was the worst place in the house," Stacey agreed.

"I think there are different ghosts that play with the games," I said.

"Noah and Luke?"

"If I see them, I'll ask." I double-checked my toolbox for all the gear I might need, then started inside.

"Testing," Stacey said over my headset as I approached the back door of the house.

"Copy," I replied. Because we talk like that sometimes.

The Pauldings had gone to bed. I sat down in a comfortable overstuffed chair in a corner of the living room, right behind the thermal and night vision cameras so I could watch their display screens. My job was to stay quiet, observe, and hope for a ghost or two to pass by during the night. I would make a few rounds with my Mel Meter to pass the time, looking for unusual energy or temperature patterns. In case nothing happened, I'd brought a paperback of *The Road* by Cormac McCarthy, because I'd been meaning to read that one for a while.

I didn't get to read much, though, because a few things did happen, and they weren't altogether pleasant.

Chapter Seven

Sometimes when I do overnight observations, I bring an inflatable mattress or sleeping bag to kind of camp out in the house. This is usually because I'm in some creepy basement or some long-neglected room where the ghost has taken up residence.

The Paulding house was already so jammed full of antique furniture accumulated over the generations, though, that it seemed absurd to bring in one more item. I was perfectly happy to take the corner chair in the living room, which was so big that I could comfortably sit cross-legged in it.

I made a few rounds of the first and second floor, noting EMF spikes right around the door to Juniper's room. Maybe it was the poltergeist or another spirit, but it wasn't doing much to make itself known so far.

The electromagnetic readings spiked again when I peeked into the crafts room with the unused sewing machine and overflowing closets. The room was cold and filled me with dread, but I didn't see anything happening in there.

The action really started at about one in the morning. I was back in the living room, and I heard a thud somewhere far above.

"Did you hear that?" Stacey asked over my headset.

"I heard something go bump in the night," I replied. "Did you see anything?"

"The attic. A cardboard box toppled off a stack of boxes and landed on the floor. Saw it on night vision. It was right next to that old rocking horse."

"Anything else happening up there?" I asked.

"I think I saw...wait, let me back up the video...yep. A little orb sailed through the box right as it fell. Just a tiny circle, like the size of a penny. Nothing else...wait. Now there's something on thermal. It's a cluster of little cold spots, blue spots. Not really a cloud, just a jumble. It's moving toward the attic stairs." Stacey gasped a little. "I think I picked up something on audio."

"What did you hear?"

"A little...squeak, maybe? I'll have to analyze...oh, the cold spots are gone now, Ellie. They drifted down the stairs."

I sat upright in my chair. "Where are they going now?"

"I can't see anything yet. Watching the hallway cam now...here they come. They passed right through the attic door. They're...uh-oh."

"What, Stacey?"

"They just went into Crane's room. We don't have a camera in there."

I stood up, but then Stacey spoke again.

"They came back out already. It looks like they're moving toward the main stairs," she said.

I walked to the living room door and peeked out. On the second of the three flights of steps, a dim figure flicked across the window, barely visible for an instant and then gone. It seemed like a pale, thin, short person.

"It's on the steps," I whispered.

The front hall where I stood grew noticeably colder. My trusty Mel Meter confirmed something was happening—the temperature dropped four degrees, and I saw exactly the same kind of electrical anomalies I'd observed in the attic. They were short, strong pulses of five to six milligaus each.

I heard something like a whisper. The entity was halfway along the first-floor hall now, and it seemed to be approaching me.

I gripped my flashlight just in case.

The whispering sounded again, much closer, and I felt a cool breeze brush against me, rustling my shirt. I jumped back, but I kept my flashlight off. No need to panic just yet.

"Ellie, the cold spots moved into the living room," Stacey whispered in my ear. "I think they're going for the games."

I stepped in front of the nearest camera, the one pointed at the downstairs powder room, and gave Stacey a nod and a thumbs-up. I didn't want to speak out loud and startle our ghost into leaving. It seemed to tolerate or ignore me for the moment. Ghosts aren't always conscious of your presence—they can easily get completely absorbed in their own activities.

I returned to the living room and did my best to skirt around the walls, weaving through furniture on my way back to my chair. The board games sat out on a coffee table in the middle of the room, near the high-powered microphone.

Easing into my chair, I looked at the little display screens of the thermal and night cameras mounted on their tripods, pointed right at the game boards. On the thermal, I saw the patch of cold blue motes Stacey had been talking about. They converged around the board games and grew denser, bits of coldness drawing together into larger blue spots.

On the *Candy Land* game board, the red player token, smiling and cartoony with its hand upraised in eternal greeting, advanced without regard to the brightly colored squares of the path, sliding heedlessly through the Lollipop Woods and directly to Candy Castle without even bothering to pass through Molasses Swamp.

The red player flopped onto its face, then flew off the board and landed on a chaise lounge halfway across the room, as if someone had thrown it.

Giggling voices sounded from the coffee table, and the cloud of cold dots condensed into two small, blurry figures on the thermal.

Two ghosts. I thought these might be Luke and Noah, the boys who had drowned and now seemed to be reaching out to seven-year-old Crane, who refused to tell me anything about them at all. I could not see anything as distinct as facial features—even their hands looked like shapeless mittens on the thermal camera. Of course, I hadn't seen any pictures of Luke and Noah Ridley from when they were alive, either, so I had no way of knowing how they'd looked.

They didn't seem particularly menacing, but that didn't stop icy dribbles of fear from creeping up my spine. Living creatures, including dogs and cats, have an instinctive negative reaction to encountering the spirits of the dead. It's a good instinct to have, because the bad ghosts can do truly horrifying things.

The *Monopoly* money Stacey and I had carefully counted out according to the rules—fifteen hundred bucks per player—now erupted into the air above the *Monopoly* board. The brightly colored bills rained down like confetti, and the otherworldly child voices laughed again.

The ghosts of young kids might seem harmless, but you can't count on that. The bad ghosts are stuck in some kind of psychological hell. Otherwise they wouldn't be here, they would move on. A person who was basically innocent in life can mutate into something twisted and dark over years of existing as a restless ghost. It's true of children, too—a little kid who was just a bit mischievous when alive might turn into a dangerous prankster ghost, one who thinks it's funny to push people down stairs or knock over a ladder when you're standing on top of it. Murder can be just another game to them.

Knowing this, I intended to proceed with caution.

The blue boy-shapes on the thermal camera grew clearer as they played, becoming a little sharper at the extremities. On the night vision camera, I saw a pair of little orbs appear over the *Monopoly* board and vanish into the wheelbarrow and dog tokens, which then raced each other across the board, tumbled off the coffee table, and landed on the rug. The orbs had been about the size of the boys' fingertips, which they seemed to represent.

"Ellie?" Stacey said over the headset. "Hey, Ellie? Ellie?"

I scowled. She should have known I wouldn't want to speak and draw the ghosts' attention. She would have been watching the feeds from the two cameras in front of me, and I assumed she was getting overexcited about it.

"Ellie?" she said again.

"What?" I finally whispered, sounding just as annoyed as I felt.

On the thermal camera, the blue boy-shapes fell suddenly still. Great. My voice had disturbed them.

Over my headset, I thought I heard Stacey say something about a bathroom.

"Did a faucet turn on?" I asked. That would indicate a third entity getting active, maybe the poltergeist, maybe somebody else.

"Not the bathroom," Stacey replied. "I said something's happening in the *bad* room. You know, the sewing room? Serious temp drop there, like down to forty-six, forty-five degrees. And I can see him on night vision, Ellie. I mean, just an outline, a green shadow surrounded by green and black--"

"What's he doing?" I whispered. The two boy figures trembled strangely on the thermal screen. If I didn't shut up, I was going to chase them away.

"He just...opened the door. Now I lost sight of him. The hallway's turning dark blue, though, and I mean he's going through there like an ice-cold thundercloud—"

A heavy footstep echoed from the front hall.

On the thermal camera, the two blue boy-shapes raced up into the air above the coffee table, moving all at once as if they'd been sucked away by some paranormal vacuum cleaner.

I looked at the night vision camera in time to see a pair of pale orbs, each as big as a bicycle training wheel, fly into the ceiling and vanish. I'd lost both ghosts.

"Where did they go?" I whispered.

"Right back to the attic," Stacey answered. "They're shrinking away into the corners there. It's like they're hiding."

I thought I saw a discolored area on the ceiling where they'd vanished. I walked over to the coffee table and looked up. A big, wet circular patch was spreading there.

A thick drop of scummy, foul-smelling water splatted against my cheek, and I quickly wiped it away. The plumbing wasn't leaking through the ceiling at all—the boy ghosts were leaving pond-water snail-trails behind.

"Ellie," Stacey said, her voice trembling. "The cold is spreading downstairs, fast. I think it's coming your way. It's like a purple-black fog. It's freezing."

He was staring at me from the doorway.

The man was tall and barrel-chested, his entire form wrapped in shadow. I felt a wave of dread like the one I'd felt in the crafts room upstairs, but it was worse now, more charged, like disaster was imminent.

He walked into the room, his face so encrusted with dirt that I couldn't make out his features. I could hear him breathing, though. His breaths were deep and ragged, with a strange whistling sound when he exhaled.

"Ellie, he's right there. Do I need to come in? I'm coming in," Stacey whispered.

I shook my head just slightly, so she could see my answer on the camera.

Then, in a blink, he was across the room, standing on the opposite side of the coffee table from me. I couldn't have moved if I'd wanted—fear had locked up every nerve and joint in my body, trapping me in place less than four feet from the apparition. I was seeing it with my bare eyes, no special goggles or cameras needed.

I studied the dark figure as he looked over the game boards and pieces. I had no choice but to stare at him, really—I didn't even want to breathe for fear the tiniest movement would draw his attention to me.

He wore an old-fashioned gentleman's coat with tails, but everything was crusted over with dark earth, from his shoes to his face. The room grew darker, as if a black cloud had passed in front of the moon outside, absorbing the pale light.

Intense cold seemed to radiate from him, as if he were an enormous block of ice chilling the room. Of course, cold doesn't actually radiate. In reality, he was drawing all the ambient heat out of the room, feeding on it for energy.

He raised his dirt-encrusted right hand over the game boards, palm down, almost as though he intended to say a benediction over Marvin Gardens. He said nothing.

A long, narrow organic shape, almost like a tongue, extended out of his hand toward the game boards. It was leathery, and despite the lifelike way it nosed among the scattered pink bank notes, I slowly realized that it was a kind of bizarre belt. Sharp buckles, prongs, plates, and hooks jutted out all over it, like some kind of awful torture whip from a dungeon museum.

The shadow man raised his arm, then brought the belt down on the game board with a crack. The belt grew as long as a bullwhip, sprouting new buckles and prongs all along the way, the metal gleaming in what remained of the moonlight.

He swept his belt-whip back and forth, and it snapped like a snake, its buckles jingling as it knocked the game boards and all the pieces onto the floor, as if this ghost were out for vengeance against Uncle Pennybags and King Kandy.

When all trace of the games had been removed from the coffee table, he fell still, and again I could hear his heavy, uneven breathing.

Then his head tilted up toward the wet green stain on the ceiling. I heard a sound that reminded me of a dog sniffing a dead animal.

His head lowered, and he looked at me.

In a blink, he was standing on my side of the table, less than a foot away from me. I could hear his breath, but I couldn't smell him at all, for which I should probably count myself lucky. He looked like a corpse that had clawed its way free of the earth. From this distance, I saw the right side of his head was misshapen, as if part of it had caved in.

Now he was staring right at me with the empty pits of his eyes.

My heart pounded in my ears. I wanted to scream. You never get used to seeing monsters like that.

With as little movement as I could, I tilted the lens of my flashlight toward his head and lay my finger on the power button.

He raised his right hand with the long, buckle-studded belt, and I had a feeling he meant to whip me with it.

I turned on my flashlight, blasting a narrow three-thousand-lumen beam right at his head. His heavy breathing turned to a choking, gagging sound as the concentrated light struck him full force.

His whip arm twitched, jangling all the metal pieces on the elongated belt.

I widened the iris of my flashlight lens, bathing him in a flood of light. A wet, angry snarl gurgled in his throat, and he slowly turned away from me.

As he rotated, I saw a hole in the left side of his head. I could see all the way through it, right through his head. I thought of Isaiah Ridley, dead of a gunshot wound.

He kept turning away, and he was kind of turning inward, twisting in on himself in the relentless glare of my light. Then he was gone. Into the gray zone where we couldn't follow, maybe, or perhaps getting ready to leap at me from another angle.

I turned back and forth, widening the iris even more so my flashlight was more like a searchlight.

"Ellie?" Stacey whispered.

"I think he's gone," I said. "It's getting warmer in here."

"What did you see?" she asked.

"What did *you* see?" I asked her in return.

"A huge cold spot...like a column of cold, eight feet high, purple and black. On the night vision, it seemed like some kind of silhouette, fading in and out."

"I saw him, full apparition," I told her. "I think it's Isaiah. And I don't think he's friendly."

Chapter Eight

Gord was the first member of the household to awaken. At about six a.m., he rolled out of his first-floor bedroom and into the kitchen to brew some coffee. He invited Stacey and me to join him. I accepted but tried not to drink too much, since I was hoping for a nap at my apartment this morning. I figured a few sips of coffee wasn't going to stop that from happening.

"How did it...go?" he asked, while Stacey and I sat at the kitchen table with him.

I gave him a quick summary of what we'd seen, including what we'd discovered about the ceiling "leaks" and the two figures who'd played with the board games. Stacey opened her laptop to show him the relevant bits of video—the thermal images of the boy-sized ghosts, the little orbs moving the game pieces.

"We've figured out the wet spots on the ceiling, at least," I said. "These two ghosts leave them behind when they travel between the floors. I think they were running from another ghost, the one upstairs in the crafts room. We caught some glimpses of him on camera, but I saw him in person. He...doesn't seem very nice."

"Who doesn't seem nice?" Toolie walked into the room wearing a blue pantsuit, full make-up, and a tag that identified her as a manager at Sir Sleepmore Mattresses. "I saw somebody made a mess in the living room."

"Two ghosts did that," I said. "I think they might be your son's invisible friends."

"Are they dangerous?" Toolie poured herself a cup of coffee.

"It's too early to tell, but they didn't act that way," I said. "On the other hand, there's a ghost in that room upstairs--"

"Stop!" a boy's voice snapped, and I jumped a little in my seat.

Crane stood at the open door to the dining room, wearing Buzz Lightyear pajamas. His hair stuck up in clumps, and he stared at me with dark, angry eyes.

"Crane? How long...have you been there?" Gord asked.

"You have to leave," Crane said, staring at me with a fairly creepy intensity for a seven-year-old.

"That's very rude, Crane!" Toolie said. "You apologize."

"They're making it worse." Crane looked from me to Stacey.

"Making what worse, Crane?" Stacey asked, in the measured tone of a guidance counselor.

"All of it. Noah and Luke say you're making him mad."

"Making who mad?" I asked.

Crane glared at me, then stomped away into the dining room.

"Crane! Come back and apologize to these ladies!" Toolie called after him.

"No!" he shouted from somewhere deeper in the house. I heard his footsteps stomping up the stairs.

"I am so sorry," Toolie said. "We've all been snapping at each other lately..."

"No need to apologize," I told her. "Anyway, it looks like his invisible friends really might be ghosts. That's more than a kid should have to deal with." I'm really defensive about kids having to face the supernatural, probably because of my own history. I hate to see ghosts stalking or threatening children.

"Oh, goodness," Toolie said. She glanced at the time on the microwave. "I need to get to work, but I want to hear more..."

"We'll be back later this afternoon," I said. We'd also caught some poltergeist activity in Juniper's room, but there wasn't time to go into that. "We can go over everything then."

A big crash sounded upstairs, followed by a scream, startling everyone. Stacey, Toolie, and I ran upstairs to find Juniper in her room, sitting up in bed. Her bookshelves had toppled over, spilling paperbacks and comic books everywhere. The shelves were only about four feet high, but they were heavy enough to do some damage if they'd landed on somebody's leg or foot.

"Are you hurt? What happened?" Toolie ran to embrace her daughter.

"What do you think?" Juniper pointed at the shelves. "That could have killed me!"

"Were you asleep?" I asked.

"Yeah. I guess I'm up now." Juniper sighed. "It was so loud."

"I wish I wasn't running late for work..." Toolie said.

"We'll help her straighten this up, Mrs. Paulding," I said.

"Oh, thank you," Toolie said, sounding genuinely grateful. "Junie, call me at work in a couple of hours, will you?"

Juniper nodded, still staring at the mess made by her possible poltergeist.

Stacey and I hung around long enough the heave the bookshelves back against the wall. Fortunately, Juniper didn't worry about organizing or alphabetizing her books at all, so it didn't take long to clean up the fallen books.

We got out of there as quickly as we could, because precious sleep time was dribbling away. We left our cameras and microphones turned off but still set up for the following night.

"What do you think?" Stacey asked me as we drove away.

"I think they have a ghost or two."

"Duh." She looked at me expectantly. I'd given her a brief idea of the shadowy man I'd encountered in the living room, but she could obviously tell I'd held something back. Now that we were out of earshot of our clients and their children, Stacey clearly wanted the gory details.

I quickly recounted the man and his bizarre belt-whip loaded with a crazy number of buckles and prongs, and how he'd used the whip to angrily slap the games off the table.

"No wonder the two kid ghosts ran away," Stacey said. "Maybe they're afraid of him. I can't believe you stayed in there by yourself the rest of the night."

"I feel more comfortable with you out here in the van, monitoring the whole house for me," I said. "I think you're right about the two ghosts. If they're Noah and Luke, and Whippy McHalf-Face is Isaiah, that would mean they're in fear of their father.

The belt would be an extension of his will to punish, probably representing something he used in life."

"So...you're saying he used to beat the boys with a belt when they were alive?"

"Possibly. And now they're caught repeating that drama after death."

"For a hundred and sixty years," Stacey said, looking a little distraught at the idea. "That's terrible."

"And it must have grown worse and worse," I said. "Isaiah's turned into this monstrous entity with a crazy weapon. The belt's grown link by link over the years, like Jacob Marley's chains."

"So creepy," Stacey whispered. "So what about the two boys? How would they have changed over the years, suffering that?"

"I don't know. They could be dangerous by now, too. But so far all we've seen them do is play with toys and run away in fear. Maybe they threw some Christmas ornaments down the attic stairs. They don't seem malevolent so far. Mischievous, I'd say."

"It must be awful for them," she said. "Like a prison, but it's worse than a life sentence. You don't get to escape even when you're dead."

"If we can find any evidence that Isaiah whipped or abused his kids in life, that would really help tie this together," I said. "At least we're getting some insight about what's going on in that house. And here's *your* house." I stopped at the curb in front of a three-story U-shaped brick building with a few of its exterior walls covered with carefully groomed mats of ivy. The apartment building was a short walk from the College of Art and Design campus and inhabited entirely by students. "Any plans to move now that you've graduated?" I asked.

"Why, do you want a roommate?" She cast her smile on me. She had an easy, charming smile that I wish I could copy. My smiles always make me look like I'm scowling, or else working up the steam to bite your head off about something. Which I'm not. Usually.

"I already have a roommate," I said.

"You have a cat."

"The two of us barely fit into the apartment at the same time," I said. I had a narrow little brick studio in a somewhat-refurbished factory loft.

"I haven't thought about it. My lease runs a couple more weeks...so...maybe I should. Because I'm adult now, not a college kid.

Totally an adult. It's weird, because I still don't feel like it."

"You still don't *act* like it, either," I said, and she stuck out her tongue before climbing out of the van.

I had enough time to drive home, feed my cat, and lie on the bed for twenty minutes before my phone woke me up. I'd forgotten to turn the ringer off. It usually doesn't matter, because I don't have tons of people calling to chat, and most of the ones who do call are trying to sell me magazine subscriptions or something.

"Grant, it's my bedtime," I said when I answered the phone. It was Grant Patterson, my usual contact at the Savannah Historical Association.

"Are you busy?" Grant asked.

"Just going to sleep," I said, thinking I'd already hinted pretty strongly at that when I'd told him it was my bedtime.

"Are you having insomnia, too? I've hardly slept this week."

"I'm sorry to hear that."

"Have you ever tried Ambien? I'm considering it," he said.

"I don't have insomnia, Grant. I spend my nights chasing ghosts in creepy old mansions." My cat Bandit jumped on top of me, purring and bashing his head into my face, so I gave him a petting.

"A fantastic job description," Grant said. "Enviable."

"Yeah, it's a real resume-stuffer," I said. Between Grant and Bandit, I gave up sleeping and sat up in bed. "Did you find something about the house?"

"My loss of sleep is your gain, dear," Grant said. "I let myself into the Association archives last night, and after thumbing through index after index, I did find a few items that should interest you. There are a number of boring public records about Isaiah Ridley's business and political activities, but one box is particularly tantalizing."

"So tantalize me, what is it?"

"Letters and family records, including correspondence from one Catherine Ridley—your woman who drowned along with her children—sent to her sister in Port Royal. Including the last several weeks of her life."

Grant hesitated, in a way that usually meant he had more gossip but needed more attention before he would relinquish it.

"That's an amazing find," I said.

"I think you'll find her final letters *very* interesting, Ellie."

"Why? What's in them?"

"They are the thoughts of an increasingly distraught woman, suffering the terrible strain of her husband's death, and finding her home...disturbed by inexplicable events," Grant said.

"Haunted?" I asked.

"Oh, yes. You'll have to come and read the letters for yourself. They cannot be removed from the archives."

"Can they be photocopied?"

"I am a research fellow, not a copy boy," Grant said. "There's a good bit of material, so come and see what you want. Visit me in my domain."

"All right. Wait. We have to test this girl for psychic powers this afternoon."

"I'm sure there's something similar on my schedule."

"Can we meet at the archives at...about seven? Ish?" I asked.

"You assume I have no plans for the evening?" Grant asked, but he sounded amused rather than annoyed.

"Seven p.m. sounds a little early for you."

"True. I'm not quite among the early-bird-special crowd just yet. Give me a few more years..."

"Thanks. That should give us time to see our clients first."

"Do what you must. I'll be here, attempting to put this box of letters into something resembling chronological order."

"I really appreciate it, Grant. Can't wait to see you." Not as much as I couldn't wait to sleep, though.

"I'm sure it will be delightful, dear."

After he hung up, I closed my eyes. I immediately saw the big, shadowy man, encrusted in dirt, half his face misshapen by the lead ball of an old-fashioned pistol, probably a flintlock. The whip writhing in his hands like a serpent, its buckles jangling. The entire room turning ice cold around him.

It seemed clear to me that, of the ghosts infesting our clients' home, Isaiah was the one we needed to worry about the most.

Chapter Nine

Eckhart Investigations is located in an industrial area a few miles west of the actual city, next to a junkyard where they crush old cars. It's in a cinderblock building we share with a couple of other shady businesses. Well, I'd like to think we're not shady ourselves, but plenty of people treat us like scam artists. Lots of folks just don't believe in ghosts until one is in their house, creeping into bedrooms and smashing Hummel figurines.

I arrived there in the middle of the afternoon to find Calvin, my boss, in the big workshop in the back of our office, loading boxes into the back of his truck. Calvin is a retired police detective, paraplegic and stuck in a wheelchair. He drives a big old forest-green Chevy Blazer with a camper shell over the truck bed.

"I said I'd help," I told him.

"Too late," he said. He wheeled around to the driver's seat. Calvin wore a tie, which was extremely unusual for him, but I guess he didn't get out much in the professional sense anymore.

He opened the door and hauled himself up into the driver's chair, refusing my attempts to help him. "If you want to help, fold up my chair and shove it in back," he said.

By the time I did that and closed up the tailgate, Calvin was already positioned in his seat, the engine rumbling, his hand on the accelerator handle. The truck had been modified to enable him to drive without his legs.

He pressed the remote clipped to his sun visor and the garage door rattled up behind us. "Now, fill me in," he said as he backed out.

I told him everything we'd observed the night before.

"You're still thinking poltergeist?" he asked.

"Maybe. Stacey recorded some movement in Juniper's room last night, but I don't think she's analyzed it very thoroughly yet. Little stuff on the dresser or floor would move around, and Juniper would stir in her sleep. We were kind of distracted by the three actual ghosts we saw."

"Sounds to me like you've got a couple of missing ghosts," Calvin said.

"What do you mean?"

"The wife and the girl. No sign of them?"

"Not so far..."

"If the father and boys are haunting the place, and the mother and daughter died in the same way alongside them, there's a good chance they're still around, too."

"We're definitely keeping our eyes open."

Calvin drove too fast into town, as he typically did, probably because of all his years as a police detective who didn't really have to worry about speeding tickets. Or maybe it was compensation for his inability to walk.

He slowed down as we reached the downtown area, heavy with pedestrians and bicyclists. It was about three-thirty when he pulled into the driveway of the old Georgian mansion. The unwanted, stagnant little pond at the center of the backyard seemed a bit larger to me, and a swarm of nasty mosquitoes hovered over it.

I grabbed the wheelchair for him. After Calvin lowered himself into it, we approached the back doors on the brick patio, since that meant I didn't have to haul Calvin backwards up the front steps. I can do that, as long as I don't mind a sore back for a couple of days.

I introduced Calvin to our clients—Toolie, Gord, Juniper. Crane was nowhere to be seen; apparently he preferred to be barricaded in his room, away from everyone. I was worried about the kid, even more so than Juniper. Who knew what the ghosts of Noah and Luke wanted with him? Maybe just a playmate, but I felt uncomfortable with the boy's situation. It didn't help that he didn't want to talk about it beyond telling us to go away.

"Do you give a lot of these tests?" Juniper asked Calvin, eyeing him warily.

"I've done my share," he said. They waited in the dining room, on opposite sides of the tables, while I brought in the boxes of testing materials, including an automatic shuffler for the Zener cards.

"Do most people turn out to be psychic, or not?" Juniper asked.

"Almost nobody does," Calvin told her.

Juniper gave a half-smile at that. "Do you think I am?"

"I'll tell you my opinion in about two hours," he said.

I set a wide, tall balsa-wood divider on the table between them. I would slide it into place at the beginning of the test so Juniper wouldn't be able to see the cards.

Stacey arrived, very conveniently, just after I'd finished carrying everything inside. She'd driven separately.

"Isn't this exciting?" Stacey asked Juniper, who responded to Stacey's overflowing enthusiasm with a half-hearted shrug. Stacey set up a camera behind Calvin, at a slight angle, to capture the cards on video as he drew them from the shuffler.

"Are you going to show this to people?" Juniper asked, frowning at the camera.

"It's just for our records," Stacey said, while setting up a high-powered microphone near the head of the table.

"Someone has to double-check the accuracy of my notes, especially at my age," Calvin said, and that actually made Juniper smile a little.

"So you're a ghost detective, too, right?" Juniper asked.

"He's the *boss* ghost detective," Stacey said. "We both work for him."

"How did you get to be one of those?" Juniper asked him.

"I used to be a city homicide detective," he said. "I ran into more than one case that turned out to involve ghosts, and that led me to research them. After a while, other investigators would bring me their 'oddball' cases. I developed a sort of unwanted reputation for solving the ghostly ones."

"So the ghosts were *killing* people?" Juniper's eyes widened. Oops, Calvin was freaking her out.

"That's very rare, I promise," he said, trying to put her at ease.

"Do you think the ghosts here will kill me?" she asked.

"I don't think so," he said, but he had no basis for saying that. Not after Whippy McHalf-Face and his Belt of Doom had put in their appearance. "We're going to get rid of your ghosts, so you don't need to worry about a thing."

Juniper didn't look like she believed him.

"Do poltergeists kill people?" she asked.

"Poltergeists are usually just pests," he told her.

"If I'm making the poltergeist, how do I stop doing it?"

"They feed on unbalanced emotions—anger, fear, hatred," Calvin said. "We usually prescribe a regular activity that will keep your energy calm and centered. You can study meditation at the Zen center, or take yoga or ta'i chi at several places around town."

"That doesn't sound so bad," Juniper said. I wondered what she'd been imagining. An elaborate exorcism, maybe.

"I know a great place for hot yoga! I've done it once, and it was awesome!" Stacey volunteered. I knew a good place, too—I went twice a week, just to keep myself sane—but it was small and out of the way, and I didn't want to run into clients there if I didn't have to, so I didn't mention it.

"It's a good practice, anyway," I offered. "Good for your health."

"Are we ready to begin?" Calvin asked, opening a small cardboard box beside him.

"I guess." Juniper gave a partial shrug.

He passed her a laminated sheet with five symbols on it.

"Each card has one of those symbols," he told her, while feeding a couple of decks into the automated shuffler. "Wavy lines, circle, square, star, or a cross. You won't be able to see me, so each time I draw a card, I'll ring this." Calvin touched the button on the sort of little bell you might find on the front desk at a hotel. It gave off a little *ding*. "Any questions?"

"Nah, sounds easy." Juniper looked over the five symbols from which she had to choose. "So I'm trying to read your mind?"

"Exactly right." Calvin nodded.

"Do I concentrate really hard, or what?"

"You can just relax," he said. "Say whatever comes to your mind."

"You'll be fine, sweetie," Toolie said. She stood in the doorway to the main hall, watching us set up in the dining room.

"I *know*," Juniper replied, looking annoyed.

"Everyone clear the room now." Calvin nodded at me, and I slid the tall balsa-wood divider into place, separating Calvin and Juniper.

Stacey, Toolie, and I walked over to the kitchen, where Gord was already sitting and watching Stacey's laptop. On the screen, we could see Calvin and the card he'd drawn. It had a circle on it.

"Star?" Juniper guessed. We couldn't see her, but the microphone picked up her voice.

Calvin made an "X" on his worksheet to indicate a wrong answer, then dropped the card back into the shuffler and drew another, which had the wavy lines on it. He dinged the little bell.

"Uh...square?" Juniper guessed. She was not off to a very accurate start.

She got the third one wrong, too.

"She doesn't seem very...psychic to me," Gord breathed.

"While the kids are busy, we wanted to catch you up on some details from last night," I told Toolie and Gord. I glanced around to make sure Crane wasn't eavesdropping from some little nook—the kid moved as quietly as a ninja. "Stacey, can you pull up one of the poltergeist videos from Juniper's room?"

"Of course." Stacey opened a second laptop and drew up a few clips of interest she'd put aside to show our clients.

On the screen, we saw Juniper asleep in bed. After a few seconds, the clothes and jewelry heaped carelessly on her dresser shifted, as if someone had pushed them, and a few items fell to the floor.

"That kind of thing happens all the time," Toolie said. "I'm always on her to clean up her room, but it can't be easy when something else is always messing it up."

"Here's the same timeframe from the thermal camera," Stacey said.

The next video clip showed Juniper as a red-orange shape in her bed.

A blurry shape the size of a soccer ball appeared near her door. It was green, speckled with blue, an unfocused blob shape with no discernible face or limbs.

It rolled across Juniper's dresser like a misshapen ball, pushing and knocking items aside, only to vanish at the far end.

"I saw that! Did you see that?" Toolie asked Gord, who nodded.

"Back it up and pause it," I told Stacey. She found a frame with a decent view of the green shape, though there wasn't much to see, no details at all. "Most ghosts show up in the blue-to-black spectrum on thermal," I told our clients. "They're constantly sucking heat out of the room to power themselves. This entity is a little warmer than a ghost but, as you can see by comparing it with Juniper, still colder than a live person. Poltergeists tend to have more energy because they're regularly feeding on the living. It's usually unfocused, destructive, kinetic energy, drawn from their human host."

Toolie looked at the other laptop, where her daughter continued trying to guess the cards behind the balsa barrier.

"Poor Juniper," she said.

"We've identified four separate entities," I said. "The poltergeist is one. Two of them we believe might be Noah and Luke Ridley, because your son came up with their names without knowing the history of the house. They seem like small-scale vandals and troublemakers, but not particularly threatening as far as we know. And the fourth..." I recounted my encounter the night before, not sparing any details this time. Gord and Toolie's eyes widened, and Toolie, who'd encountered the shadow-man before, turned pale. Gord looked horrified as I described the man's long, metal-spiked torture belt.

Stacey showed the scene on her laptop. First, she ran the night vision clip, where all we could really see was the game objects moving by themselves. I pointed out the little orbs that winked in and out around the moving objects.

When the tall shadow-man arrived, it barely registered on camera. Toolie and Gord watched me stand, frozen in fear, while a vague outline of a man faded in and out of view. At one point, a greenish thread blinked over to the *Candy Land* game board to flip it off the coffee table, and that was the only hint of his bizarre weapon on the night vision.

Then Stacey played the same clip in thermal, so they could see the bluish boy-shapes and hear the snatch of laughter she'd caught on the microphone.

"My word," Toolie whispered. "Those are the boys Crane's been talking about this whole time?"

"We believe so, but we can't be one hundred percent certain yet," I said. "We're going to visit the Historical Association in a little while for some more research on the Ridley family." I checked the time. We needed to meet Grant in about an hour and a half.

On the screen, the two light blue shapes flew up into the ceiling. The shadow-man we believed to be Isaiah Ridley entered, a tall purple-black shape that filled the living room with deep blue cold.

"That's him," Toolie whispered. "Isn't it? The one I saw upstairs?"

Gord gave her a questioning look, but didn't say anything. I guessed a private conversation about Toolie's encounter would happen a bit later, when Stacey and I weren't around.

"He came from the crafts room, Mrs. Paulding," Stacey said. "I don't have that clip separated out for you yet, but I watched him open the door and walk toward the stairs. Well, he kind of drifted..."

"There was a hole in his head." I pointed to my left temple. "And the right side of his face was shattered. He was all covered in dirt, so it was hard to see very much, but that seems consistent with a man who shot himself. So I really think this is Isaiah."

"Four ghosts," Toolie said, shaking her head.

"You mean three and a...half," Gord said. "The poltergeist isn't really a...ghost."

Stacey and I smiled at his little joke, which seemed to cheer him up for the moment.

"That's right, Mr. Paulding," I said. "I have to say that I'm most concerned about Isaiah himself. Clearly, he can interact with physical objects in a forcible way. The other two ghosts, possibly his own sons, seem afraid of him. He has that odd weapon, which to me indicates he may have beaten his children with a belt. I'd like to go ahead and construct a trap for him, try to get him out of your house and on his way."

"Oh, yes, please." Toolie all but sighed the words, and she looked relieved. "Can you do that tonight?"

"Stacey and I will need to poke around in your attic," I said. "If we can find any objects of personal significance to Isaiah, it would help us bait the trap."

"Oh, yes, do what you need to do," Toolie said. "Let me know if I can help."

"Do you know if there might be anything left from the Ridley family?"

"If there is, it must be in some of those old trunks at the very back," Toolie said. "It's a mess up there. I usually only go far enough to grab the Christmas stockings or Easter baskets."

"We'll have a look," I said.

On the screen, we watched Juniper take her tests. After the Zener cards, there was a test where Calvin spun a color wheel with a pointer on one side, Wheel-of-Fortune-style, and she had to guess which color the pointer indicated when the wheel stopped. After a number of repetitions, they switched to a test involving a series of little boxes, each with an animal figurine inside, and she had to guess which animal was in which box.

Finally, there was a telekinesis test. After sliding the screen out of the way, Calvin placed one tiny object after another on the table—a shirt button, a thimble, and so on—and encouraged her to focus on them and try to move them with her mind.

None of them budged.

The testing lasted for more than an hour, after which Calvin and Juniper joined us in the kitchen. Juniper looked exhausted, like she'd just completed a thousand-page math test filled with convoluted word problems.

"How did it go?" Toolie asked. Juniper shrugged and grabbed a Sprite from the refrigerator.

"I haven't compiled all the numbers yet," Calvin said. "I'll need to add up—"

"I sucked at it," Juniper said. "I totally failed."

"There's no reason to get upset," Toolie said.

"This won't take long." Calvin added up the scores from the Zener-card test. "Since there are five cards, a score of twenty percent is considered the same as random chance. Yours was..." He tapped the numbers into his calculator. "Twenty-four point three seven...just a bit above average."

"Yay," Juniper said sarcastically, leaning against the counter. "Watch out, everybody, I'm slightly above average."

"So what does that mean?" I asked. "You don't think she's creating the poltergeist?"

"It seems less likely than before," Calvin said. "What about your other child? I understand he may have interacted with two of the ghosts."

"You mean Crane?" Toolie asked. "You think *he's* making the poltergeist?"

"I'm just gathering information," Calvin told her. "As long as I'm here, it might be a good thing for me to test him, if y'all don't mind."

"We have to meet Grant soon..." I checked the time on my phone. "Should I tell him we'll be late?"

"Let's see if I can even get Crane to work with us," Toolie said while pushing herself to her feet. "He's been in a mood lately."

"He's a little pest," Juniper said.

"Juniper, do you fight with your brother very often?" Calvin asked.

"Like feral cats and rabid dogs," Toolie muttered as she left the room.

"Well, it's his fault! He's always bugging me and trying to take my stuff," Juniper said. "I just want him to leave me alone."

"If he has some unresolved anger toward you, that could explain why the poltergeist seems to be focused on you," Calvin said.

"Whoa, wait." Juniper scowled. "You mean my little brother is attacking me with a poltergeist? I swear, I'm going to give him the worst Indian burn ever."

"It's not intentional," I said.

"If the poltergeist is drawing energy from Crane, and Crane is angry at you, it could simply be absorbing that anger. And harassing you as a result," Calvin said.

"I knew it wasn't my fault!" Juniper looked triumphant as Toolie returned with a very reluctant Crane. The seven-year-old frowned at all of us, his dark eyes odd and solemn.

"Crane, this is Mr. Eckhart, a detective," Toolie said. "He's going to play some games with you."

"Why does he want to play games with a little kid?" Crane asked. I admit, I had to bite my lip to avoid laughing.

"It's a kind of test, like in school," Toolie said. "Only you don't get a grade. Just try for me, sweetie."

Crane gave a big sigh, but he accompanied his mom and Calvin into the dining room.

Stacey and I had to leave in a few minutes, but we watched the beginning of the session along with Toolie, Gord, and Juniper, who leaned over my chair to watch over my shoulder.

"Star," Crane said on the screen, correctly identifying the card my boss had just drawn. "Waves. Square. Square. Circle."

The five of us grew silent and still. We could see the cards on the video.

"Cross. Waves." Crane said. We could hear some rustling on his side of the balsa-wood screen, but we couldn't see him. His voice grew more and more agitated. "Star! Cross! Waves!"

"Is he...?" Toolie asked, clearly unsure how to finish her sentence.

Crane had correctly identified eight of the ten cards. He kept going for three or four more, then announced "I'm done!"

"We still have a few more--" Calvin began.

"I don't want to play anymore!" We heard his footsteps thumping rapidly toward us, and then the dining-room door opened and Crane ran to his mom. "I'm all done!"

"Crane, maybe you should go back and finish," Toolie said.

"No. Luke and Noah want me to come play with them. They're in my closet." Crane dashed away. His footsteps echoed through the hall as he ran upstairs.

"That's a shame." Calvin rolled through the open door to join us.

"I'm so sorry," Toolie said. "I think he got uncomfortable."

"He said Noah and Luke called him away," I told Calvin.

"Eleven out of fourteen." Calvin shook his head. "That's about seventy-nine percent. Of course, the test is inconclusive, the sample size too small--"

"But you're thinking yes," I interrupted.

"I'm thinking yes," Calvin agreed, looking at the parents. "Added together with his apparent ability to see and hear at least two of the ghosts, I'd say your son is psychically gifted."

"Oh, come on!" Juniper snapped. "What does he have to beat me at this?"

"It's not about beating you, Junie--" Toolie began.

"It shouldn't even count! He didn't even finish the stupid test, and I sat in there forever!" Juniper gave the fed-up *ugh* grunt of a deeply annoyed teenage girl as she left the room, shaking her head.

"So..." Gord said. "Time to sign Crane up...for tai' chi?"

"It wouldn't be a bad idea at all," Calvin said. "This may get complicated, though."

"*Get* complicated?" Toolie asked. "When was it simple?"

"Poltergeists are most commonly associated with adolescent girls," Calvin said. "We can speculate about why, but that's what the data shows. Those associated with teenage boys tend be less pronounced, less high-energy, as if there's less emotional power behind them. Now, it's very rare for a child of Crane's age, seven or eight, to produce a poltergeist—but when they do...it can be unusually powerful."

"What does...that mean for us?" Gord asked.

"It still means we need Crane to stop feeding the poltergeist, through the methods we mentioned earlier, but it could take longer to accomplish," Calvin said. "If you stop feeding it, the poltergeist *will* go dormant or dissipate in time. Your boy will have to cooperate, though."

"We'll do what we can," Toolie said.

"Holy cow, we're running late, Ellie!" Stacey announced, pointing to the time on her laptop screen. "We have to meet Grant in five seconds...and....now we're late."

"Sorry, we need to run," I told them. "We'll be back tonight to observe, and to rummage around your attic." I turned to Calvin. "Are you ready to go, too?" I was really asking whether he wanted me to help him load the wheelchair into the truck again.

"As long as I'm here, I'd like to ask a few more questions," Calvin said. "And maybe we can convince the boy to come back down."

"I'll do my best." Toolie wished us well before leaving the room to go after him.

Calvin nodded at me. He could fold up his wheelchair and pull it up into the truck with him, but it was a little extra trouble.

"Okay, good luck," I said.

Stacey said cheerful good-byes to both of them. We'd had a small break in the case, at least. Maybe Grant would have something more for us.

We took Stacey's car, and she drove to the old mansion housing the Savannah Historical Association as fast as she could.

Chapter Ten

The Association occupies a three-story Federal-style mansion on Drayton Street, its front door looking out onto the sprawling lawn of Forsyth Park, the largest of the many parks downtown. It's a beautiful structure, gray brick with white and black trim, a little reminiscent of the Paulding family house but much larger, without the ornate touches of pilasters and columns. A practical place for serious scholarship. A widow's walk on the roof, surrounded by black iron railings, offers a fourth-floor view of the park and the city around it.

The house was donated to the Association by one of its founders, a woman named Mariel Lancashire, who never married or had children and spent her days fighting against demolition of the city's more historic buildings. She left the mansion in her will with the stipulation that it be devoted to "sober research and learning for the ennobling of the human spirit."

We parked on the shady side street behind the old mansion, walked through a garden planted with roses and hydrangeas in full bloom, and climbed the steps to the back porch, where we rang the rear doorbell. The Association was closed on the weekends—and wasn't open very long on weekdays, either, unless there was an event or you had an appointment. Grant, fortunately, had his own key and could come and go as he pleased.

Grant opened the door with a smile, dressed in a white summer suit with a baby-blue silk tie and matching handkerchief. In his late fifties, Grant was always spotlessly dressed and impeccably groomed, his shoes polished into black mirrors, each graying hair on his head in place as if an invisible hairdresser ghost followed him around at all times.

"Good evening, ladies," he said, stepping aside for us to enter. "Fashionably late. I approve."

"Sorry, Grant," I told him. "We were tied up with a client."

"Sounds like quite an adventure." Grant locked the back door behind us. "Worthy of Indiana Jones himself."

"Very funny. It's always so nice in here." We'd stepped into a rear gallery hung with portraits of city notables, like town founder James Oglethorpe, Girl Scout founder Juliet Gordon Lowe, writer Flannery O' Connor, and Supreme Court Justice Clarence Thomas.

The air was cool from the air conditioning, but also unusually crisp and light because of the mansion's dehumidifiers, which help preserve the vast collection of old books, maps, and papers against the heavy, damp Georgia air.

"Let's hear your story," Grant said. He led us up the back stairs, made of wide hardwood steps polished to a high gleam, much like his shoes. "I want all the spine-tingling details."

While he led us into an archive room, with shelves and shelves of paperwork stored in plastic bins surrounding a few round cherry work tables that were probably worth thousands of dollars each, I gave him some details of our current case and the ghosts we were facing.

"A poltergeist?" he asked, raising an eyebrow. "How dark and Germanic." Grant gestured to one of the tables and lifted the lid off a clear plastic tub. "I know, these plastic containers aren't as romantic as the old chests and crumbling leather valises in which the old documents tend to arrive...they're a bit Hobby Lobby, in fact...but they're much more useful for preservation."

Grant eased out a few yellowed documents, while Stacey and I sat in the high-backed chairs at the table.

"Your friend Isaiah had a busy life before it was cut short," he said, easing into the chair across from us. "Here we have a variety of legal documents...there's an investor's prospectus for the Georgia

Canal and Railroad Company, for instance...Isaiah was described as a tall man with a severe look. Fond of horse racing, apparently. Merciless in his business dealings."

"What about the letters?" I asked. "You mentioned his wife's letters."

Grant sighed. "Always trying to skip to the juicy parts. Can't I present this in my own melodramatic, drawn-out fashion?"

"Normally that would be great, but we have to get back to our clients' house and dig around in their haunted attic," I said. "I'd like to do that before sunset if we can."

"You don't have much time," Grant said, checking his watch. It was an antique wind-up, no doubt some expensive heirloom one of his ancestors had probably purchased in Switzerland. "How unfortunate for me. I wish I had clients with such interesting problems, instead of dowagers endlessly revising their wills to punish this or that grandchild." Grant is a semi-practicing attorney, trading on his old family name to do business with other old-money types in town.

"Come with us on a ghost hunt sometime," I offered.

"I'll consider it." He brought out an old folder tied with string and carefully opened it, revealing a stack of yellowed, hand-written pages. "Catherine Ridley's letters to her sister," he said. "As promised, I've made an attempt to arrange them in order. The papers were scrambled, and of course only the first page of each letter actually has the date inscribed upon it..."

"I really appreciate it, Grant," I said. "You mentioned the last letter in particular?"

"I believe it's the last letter. Towards the end, she takes less care about little niceties like dating the letters, and her handwriting grows more frantic and difficult to read." Grant pulled on latex gloves and used rubber-tipped tweezers to gently draw the last few pages out of the folder.

"What are the gloves for?" Stacey asked.

"To avoid damaging the paper with my wonderful natural oils," he said.

"Does that mean we have to wear them, too?" she asked.

"Only if you intend to touch anything in this room." Grant turned the pages to face me, then passed me the tweezers. I opened and closed them nervously while I read.

Or *struggled* to read, I should say, because Catherine's handwriting really was difficult. The faded cursive letters, leaning sharply forward as though she'd scrawled out the letter in a blind panic, weren't easy to decipher, especially on yellowing old paper. Grant clicked on the high-powered desk lamp built into the table, which was mounted on a movable mechanical support arm alongside a big magnifying glass. For just such occasions, I assumed.

"Thank you," I said, leaning forward to adjust the glass and peer through it.

"What does it say?" Stacey asked.

"You might begin with the second paragraph," Grant suggested.

The scrawled letter didn't appear to be organized into clear paragraphs, but I found what Grant was probably talking about, and I read aloud for Stacey's benefit.

"'The disturbances I described in my last letter have grown worse,'" I read. "'There has been a darkness on this house since Isaiah's death, I am sure of it, a curse of evil. I pray for relief but the Lord sends none. I told you before of the strange knocking from Isaiah's office—as though someone stood inside, requesting to be allowed out of the room. Two nights ago it began again. I took my candle and walked into the hall, thinking first to check on the children, and found them all sleeping, as though the knocking was heard only by me. I fear I may be going mad.

"'I went to Isaiah's office. The rapping had stopped by now, the house silent and cold. It has been a bitter January in so many ways for us. I opened the door, which creaked badly, as it has taken to doing in the past month. I saw nobody in there, but someone could have hidden behind his desk, or in one of his closets or cabinets.

"'I spoke—I cannot recall my specific words now, but spoke to ask if anyone was there, and that they show themselves promptly. The room was dreadfully cold, more so than the hall had been. This might owe to the lack of a fire, which I have not bothered to restore since he died, as it would entirely be a waste of fuel to warm his office now—yet it seemed cold even for that, and I checked the windows but could find no draft. The cold burned through my night clothes, into my very bones.

"It was when I inspected the windows that the voice spoke to me. It was only one word, my name, *Catherine*, but clear and loud as a branch breaking under the weight of ice in the winter. I turned and said his name, because it was his voice, you see, I knew it so well, hearing it day and night these many years. Isaiah. He spoke to me, but just that once, just that word. I searched all through the office and did not find him. I even looked in the little cabinet where Eliza used to hide, thinking she might be the one who'd done the knocking, but it was empty.

"I closed the door and have not entered the room since. There is worse to report. I told you of strange events that would happen, the dish that leaped from the table, the time Eliza's drinking glass shattered though no one had touched it. It continues, sometimes in the daylight hours as well as at night, items and furniture moving on their own as though by some restless spirit—and it seems to follow Eliza particularly. An hour before sitting to write this letter—it is night time—I heard a scream from her room.

"'I do not know how to put this in words without sounding feeble. I found Eliza in her corner, poor thing, her hair a yellow tangle, weeping and screaming, her face red and smeared with tears. She was being tormented. Toys floated before her—her favorite doll, the boys' jacks, a wooden rabbit with wheeled feet. They spun and rose and fell as through carried by some evil whirlwind, and Eliza held up her arms to protect herself.

"'I lifted the poor girl and clutched her tight—and I was deeply afraid myself—but the thing passed, and the toys dropped to the floor, as if the wind had died—but there was no wind, I promise you, and besides, what wind could do that?

"'Eliza is in my bed now, just steps away from me, asleep again by some miracle, but I do not know if I shall ever sleep in this house again. I have a mind to call on Mr. Humphries, our pastor, but fear he will only think me an hysterical woman.

"'I do not know if this spirit is truly Isaiah or not—though it was his voice I heard, he would never torment poor Eliza. He was hard on the boys, as you know, a strong believer in discipline, but he doted on the girl, in his way. He was never so rough with her. I fear it is some devil of vengeance, here to torment us all—and just when it seemed the long darkness had finally lifted. I am filled with guilt, and do not know how to live with these horrors, nor how to banish them from our home.

"'I must sleep now, but will write again soon when my wits have returned. I do hope you will keep your promise of a longer visit when the weather warms, and please give my love to all. Yours, Catherine.'"

"So, wow," Stacey said. "Isaiah started haunting them right away.

Do you think he drowned them in the pond?"

Grant looked to me, eyebrows raised in definite interest. "Do we think that?" he asked.

"I can't say," I said. I was still feeling bad for the little girl Eliza. "Well, if the crafts room is Isaiah's old office, it sounds like he's been haunting it since his death. But she says he wouldn't torment the little girl, he'd be more likely to go after the boys."

"Like he's done again and again for the past hundred and sixty years, right?" Stacey asked.

"I also wonder whether Eliza may have been dealing with a poltergeist," I said. "Something following her around, throwing objects, loose psychokinetic energy whirling through her room..."

"Wait," Stacey said, sitting up and scrunching her forehead as she thought it over. "But it wouldn't be the same poltergeist that Juniper's dealing with now, would it? Or would it?"

"That...would be a very unusual case," I said. "Poltergeists usually burn out. The emotional makeup of their creator shifts as they grow up, and even without realizing it, they've stopped feeding the poltergeist their emotional energy."

"So our advice for Juniper would just speed up that chilling-out-as-you-grow-up process?" Stacey asked.

"Right. Nothing chills you out like yoga or Zen," I said. "The average lifespan of a poltergeist is six to eighteen months. Then they just kind of dissolve from lack of energy."

"Or go dormant," Stacey said. "Right? Calvin said something about going dormant. So what if something happened to wake it up?"

"Then we'd be talking about a poltergeist that's a hundred and sixty years old," I said. "I don't know how an entity like that might grow or evolve over time, what powers it might gain, how self-aware it might become, what would motivate it..." I shook my head, overwhelmed with thoughts and possibilities. "It's still entirely possible Crane created the poltergeist himself. The boy has some psychic talent."

"He seems troubled," Stacey said. "Like really, really troubled, to me, anyway..."

"His two best friends are ghosts from the nineteenth century," I said. "That's a pretty lonely life. I hate it when kids have to deal with this kind of stuff. Life's hard enough without it." I leaned over the magnifying glass again. "Grant, do you have any of the letters leading up to this one?"

He used the tweezers to gently move the yellow papers around.

I read backwards in time, letter by letter, moving slowly as I deciphered Catherine's faded handwriting.

Her previous letter described more instances of things moving on their own, like a teapot rising from the stove and flying across the kitchen, very poltergeist-y stuff. The knocking sounds at night, a sound like moaning from the home office where her husband had died.

It wasn't hard to imagine the terrible emotional toll it must have taken on Eliza, just eight years old, her father blowing his brains out after losing all his money. The darkness that would have hung over the house. That could have been enough of an emotional crucible to make a small girl generate a poltergeist, I thought. I felt so sorry for the girl, now long dead, and the mother frantically trying to cope with unseen, ghostly forces in the house on top of all the other weight that her life had put on her—broke, three children to support, widowed in a most horrible way, her husband choosing to abandon them all for the cold comfort of the grave.

I managed to hold back some tears.

The tone and content of the letters shifted immensely when we moved backwards in time to her mid-December Christmas letter, detailing with enthusiasm her holiday preparations, new dresses she'd had made for herself and Eliza, presenting in every way the picture of a happy family. There was no hint in that letter of the horror to come.

Darker shadows appeared in her earlier letters to her sister, though. She fretted that her husband was too harsh with their boys, much too quick to punish and reprimand, that her daughter was always disappearing into hiding places around the house, and her husband was reducing the household budget yet again...In one, she mentioned how her husband had left their son Noah's legs peppered with bloody welts from his iron belt buckle.

"That fits," Stacey said, nodding. "That fits everything."

"What time is it?" I'd completely lost track. I checked my phone —we were more than an hour late. Reading through Catherine's letters had been a slow, time-eating process, but I felt like we'd picked up a few puzzle pieces for our case. It definitely confirmed for me that removing Isaiah was our top priority. If he'd abused his own children, then he could be working his way up to attacking Crane and

Juniper, too. From the letters, it sounded like Crane, as the boy, would be in greater danger.

It would have helped a great deal if we could get the kid to talk to us.

"Can we take these letters with us?" I asked Grant. "I need to study them all."

"Absolutely not," he said.

"I need to come back and make copies tomorrow, then," I said.

"I'll make them for you," Grant said.

"I thought you said you weren't a copy boy."

"I'm not, but if I were acting as a junior ghost investigator..." He smiled.

"I deputize you a junior ghost investigator," I said, mockingly gesturing on either side of his head, like a queen bestowing a knighthood, using rubber-tipped tweezers in place of a sword. Dorky, I know. "Go forth and copy." Super-dorky.

"I will proceed immediately to the fearsome Canon multi-purpose machine." He gingerly lifted the letters in his gloved hands.

We thanked him and ran out the door into a rainy evening. We'd been so engrossed in the letters, we hadn't even noticed the sound of rainfall on the roof.

Stacey drove as fast she could, but we still had to go by the office and pick up the van, and it was already dark by the time we reached our clients' haunted home.

Chapter Eleven

It was a good thing we'd set up all our gear inside the Paulding house the night before, because the rain was pounding by the time I nosed the van into their driveway. Stacey was worried the bad weather might interfere with reception to her monitors inside the van.

"Look at that." I pointed at their back yard, where the downpour sent gushers of water to collect in the low depression. It looked like a true pond now, almost a third of the grass totally flooded. "How much do you want to bet that's exactly the location of the pond where Catherine and her children drowned?"

"I told you that's where the bodies are buried," Stacey said, snickering a little. You can't do this job without developing a somewhat morbid sense of humor. Stacey's was coming along fine.

The wind and rain billowed sideways under our umbrellas, drenching us on the brief walk to our clients' front door.

"Oh, my goodness," Toolie said when she greeted us. "You look like a couple of wet kittens. Come on in. Would you like some hot tea? Or I could brew some decaf."

"If you could brew some caf, that would be better," I said. "Thank you."

She brought us towels, and Juniper came down from her room

to peer at us.

We joined Gord in the living room, where I gave a quick recount of what we'd learned from the archives. I didn't mention the outside possibility of a hundred-and-sixty-year-old poltergeist; it still seemed far more probable that Crane had created a new one. I wanted to consult with Calvin and do a little research before even broaching that subject. We were able to confirm the identity of the three non-poltergeist ghosts, though, which felt like some progress.

"I'd recommend you have keep a close eye on Crane," I told Toolie at one point. "From what we've learned, Isaiah is more likely to harm him than Junie."

"This is just awful," Toolie said, shaking her head. "Well, he's already gone to sleep tonight. This whole thing hasn't seemed to bother him too much. Not like Junie."

Juniper nodded. "It only comes after me. Like I...like it wants to bother me or hurt me for some reason."

"That's the poltergeist," I said. "Not Isaiah's ghost."

I wished my quick summary had gone a little quicker, because it was almost ten-thirty by the time Gord and Toolie finished asking questions and let us get to work. They retired to their separate bedrooms, Gord downstairs because the steps were too hard on him, Toolie upstairs to stay near her children.

Juniper hung around, watching us while Stacey swapped out the batteries in the downstairs hallway camera, the one meant to catch any activity around the powder room faucet.

"I don't feel like sleeping," Juniper said. "Can I hang out with y'all for a while?"

"Maybe," I said, unable to resist smiling a little. I have to admit, the girl kind of reminded me of a younger version of myself. She also reminded me of Grant, jokingly calling himself a junior ghost investigator. Sure, my job's all fun and games until an evil presence lurking in the cellar tries to kill you. "How well do you know your way around your attic?"

"I've been up there a few times." Juniper shrugged. "Mom makes me get the Christmas decorations and stuff."

"Good enough for me," I said.

She watched as we made our rounds of the house, changing out battery packs on the cameras and making sure they were recording. Stacey turned the cameras in the upstairs hallway to face the closed door to the crafts room so we could monitor whether Isaiah left it during the night.

The three of us shivered as we stepped into the cold crafts room itself. My Mel-Meter showed an unnatural low temperature of forty-two degrees—compared to about seventy-eight degrees in the rest of the house—and the EMF reading spiked up by eight milligaus. There could have been a dozen ghosts in that room, with readings like that. Isaiah's presence was a strong one.

We didn't speak in that room, just hurried to swap out the camera battery packs. It felt like something was watching us from the shadows, that same uncomfortable feeling you get on the back of your neck when you sense someone looking at you from behind.

We relaxed a little after leaving and closing the door.

"I hate that room," Juniper whispered. She was shaking a little. "I always have."

"For good reason," I told her, patting her on the back. "But we will help you. I promise." I felt the greater responsibility of my job at moments like these—not just nabbing ghosts and collecting a paycheck, but protecting the lives and sanity of people who've been troubled by the supernatural, especially the kids. "Maybe you shouldn't come up into the attic with us."

"I'm totally coming." Juniper straightened up. "I'm not scared of the attic."

Before heading up there, I opened my toolbox, strapped on my thermal goggles and perched them above my eyes. They're heavy, boxy things, so this is about as comfortable as duct-taping a brick to your forehead.

Stacey placed the night vision goggles, which were also pretty annoyingly cumbersome, on her head.

I opened the door to the attic, flipped on the lights and led the way upstairs, into the flickering gloom created by the dying bulb above. Juniper followed, carrying a spare tactical flashlight, and Stacey was behind her—the order was meant to keep our client safe if anything happened. The ghosts in the attic were not threatening, so far as we knew, but it's wise to be cautious.

We climbed the steep steps, emerging near one end of the attic, where an old wooden railing surrounded the stairwell area, and the heaps of old stuff extended out into the dim distance under three widely spaced bulbs overhead.

Rain pounded the roof just above us. Water dashed constantly against the high, narrow dormer windows, which brought us no light at all, not even a glimmer from a streetlamp.

I checked my Mel Meter and found similar readings as before, the EMF markedly high, the temperature low but not chilly or freezing.

"What's that?" Juniper asked, pointing to the device.

"It's a handy tool for detecting possible paranormal activity," I said. "Unexplained low temperatures and electromagnetic spikes can tell you if there might be a ghost."

"Cool. What's it telling you now?"

"The same thing it told me yesterday—there could be a presence here. From our observations last night, we're guessing it's...those two boys." I avoided saying their names. I wasn't here to stir them up or grab their attention, not at all. I much preferred they leave us alone in our rummaging.

We ducked under those annoying low beams while we walked toward the far end of the attic, where cardboard boxes gave way to wooden crates and old chests. Dust and spiderwebs were everywhere. I lowered my thermal goggles and saw a pretty unnerving number of little glowing-yellow spider bodies scattered all over the room. It seemed unusually infested, but maybe some of them had crawled inside to escape the rainstorm.

I used my flashlight to clear the little critters out of the way before Juniper or Stacey could walk into their webs.

"What are we looking for?" Juniper asked.

"Anything to do with the Ridley family, especially Isaiah Ridley. They lived here mostly in the 1840's, up until 1851, so...look for the oldest stuff you can find," I said.

Stacey and I started lifting chest lids, while Juniper opened drawers in an old bureau squatting near the back corner of the attic. The contents were jumbled, as if somebody had hastily thrown things together—a dress, a man's jacket, assorted kitchenware that looked a little bit primitive, a painted doll with yarn hair. I wondered if this was the same doll with which the poltergeist had menaced little Eliza.

"I found it!" Juniper announced. "Or some stuff with that Isaiah guy's name on it. It's mostly a bunch of papers and junk, but..." She shrugged, looking to me for a response.

"Good work," I said. "Let me take a look."

What she'd found in the old desk was mostly an assortment of Isaiah's tax papers and legal records. One drawer contained a few brochures and one-sheet ads about the failed Georgia Canal and Railroad Company. Under these, I saw something that made me smile.

I drew it out: a little iron locomotive, about as long as my finger, patchy with rust, with the insignia "GC&R" on the side.

"Here we go." I held it up in the light from the bare bulb above. "*Great* find, Juniper."

"What is it?" Stacey asked, stepping closer and lighting the little object with her flashlight.

"It looks like some kind of promotional item for the Georgia Canal and Railroad," I said. "The company that ate Isaiah's investment money. The bankruptcy may have led to Isaiah's suicide."

"Sh," somebody said.

"What?" I looked at Juniper.

"Huh? I didn't say anything," Juniper said.

"Me, either," Stacey said, glancing around. "I heard it, though. Right after you mentioned Isaiah's death--"

"*Sh,*" the voice repeated, and it definitely wasn't Stacey or Juniper this time, because I could see them both.

"What was that?" Juniper whispered.

The three of us shined our flashlights around the attic, our beams crossing back and forth over the old furniture and storage chests.

I saw something flicker for a moment, but it was just a shadow on the wall. I thought it was my own shadow, cast by somebody else's flashlight. Then the shadow turned and stepped behind a tall, dusty bookshelf, out of the glare of my light. Goose bumps rose all over my skin.

"Noah? Luke?" I asked, which made Stacey and Juniper turn their heads. "Who's there? I saw you. We're not here to cause you any trouble--"

"*Sh!*" the voice sounded a third time, louder and more insistent now, enough to make Stacey jump.

"What the cow?" Stacey asked, pointing her flashlight in the direction of the voice.

The flickering light over the stairs finally went out, leaving only two bulbs to push against the deep gloom. Then the light bulb at the center of the room crackled and fell dark, followed by the final bulb, the one closest to us, leaving us with only our flashlights for illumination.

"What's happening?" Juniper asked.

"*Sh,*" sounded a fourth time, but now it was very quiet, hardly audible at all.

A footstep fell on one of the attic stairs, and the wooden step seemed to groan under the weight of a large person.

The attic grew cold. I could feel the freezing air hit me like a moving wall, and I saw Stacey and Juniper wince a little as it struck them, too.

"What do we--?" Juniper began.

"Sh," I told her, then I whispered, "That was me that time."

I pulled the thermal goggles down over my eyes.

The room was so deep blue, it looked like we were underwater. A dark purple head, mottled with black, rose up from the steps and peered right at me through the railing. I could feel it staring, just as I'd felt it down in the crafts room.

Now I understood why Noah and Luke's ghosts might be shushing us. They didn't want us drawing Isaiah's attention up to the attic, which seemed to be the boys' domain.

Oops.

I jabbed my flashlight in Isaiah's direction, trying to punch him through the head with a solid blast of white. It seemed to work—he actually ducked down out of sight. The attic still felt like the inside of a refrigerator.

With gestures, I told Stacey to accompany me and Juniper to stay put. Juniper nodded with wide eyes, clutching her flashlight. If I had to risk either leaving Juniper with the boy ghosts or bringing her closer to Isaiah and his crazy torture belt, the choice was obvious to me.

Stacey and I advanced across the attic, the floorboards creaking beneath us. My heart was thumping somewhere near my esophagus as we approached the railing and leaned over for a look. We shined our flashlights down onto the two flights of steps below.

As far as we could see, there was nothing. The air was cold and blue in my thermal goggles, but there was no dense concentration of cold, no purple-black mass in the shape of a large man.

I lifted my goggles away to look with my own eyes. Dusty stairs, nothing more.

Stacey breathed out a little sigh of relief.

"Looks like he stepped out," she whispered. "Maybe into the gray zone?"

"Maybe."

"What's the gray zone?" Juniper asked. Despite the fairly clear instructions I'd given with my hands, she'd tiptoed after us and now stood just halfway across the attic instead of at the far end. I shined my light into the shadows around her, checking for any trouble.

"The gray zone isn't really a definite thing," I explained. "It's just our word for where ghosts go when we can't track them down--"

Something snatched my ankle. Fingers as sharp as vulture talons dug into my boot.

I was pulled backwards by a great force, right off my feet. The old railing cracked and shattered beneath me, no more sturdy than if had been made of toothpicks and popsicle sticks.

I fell through and into the empty space over the stairs. I seemed to hover there, just a moment, like Wile E. Coyote after running off a cliff...then I dropped hard onto the steps below, banging my knee, hip, ribs, and head against the stairs. My flashlight clattered away in a swoop of light, rolling down the steps and across the landing below.

I had landed upside down on the stairs, my feet near the top step, my head pointed down toward the landing. The impact knocked the air from my lungs, and I couldn't move.

That moment of breathless paralysis seemed to stretch on and on, as if I were in a place where time barely flowed at all.

A heavy footstep clomped on the stair just below my head. The air turned so cold it seemed to freeze solid around me.

I craned my neck back, rolling my eyes up to see him. From where I lay, he seemed like a giant, crusted in filth and dark earth, head half-collapsed, like a pumpkin two weeks after Halloween. The long belt quivered in his hand, its crust of buckles and studs clacking together like metallic teeth.

With my head thrown back like that, my throat was dangerously exposed, only inches from the cluster of long, sharp prongs at the tip of the belt. If he hit me as hard as I'd seen him strike the game boards in the living room, he could kill me right there.

I urged the muscles in my arms and legs to move, but they remained useless, as if flash-frozen into place by the rapid temperature drop. His raspy breathing continued. Ghosts don't need to breathe. It was a sign of mental disorder on his part, a failure to fully accept his own death.

I felt as if I lay on a frozen tundra somewhere near the Arctic, with a beast hungry for meat and blood pinning me down and sniffing at my neck. All I could hear was my own heartbeat, nothing else. The rest of the world had fallen silent.

Isaiah leaned forward and peered at me, his eyes sunken deep in their sockets, giving them a hollow look. I could smell him now, sour earth and decay, and I could have gagged. I could taste him in the back of my throat like a pungent splash of chunky sour milk.

The belt crawled onto my face like a rotten, leathery millipede with sharp steel legs. Its prongs poked at my cheek.

I heard shouting voices, Stacey and Juniper, but they sounded distant and tinny to me, as though I were listening to them from the far end of a long, echoing pipe.

I felt like I'd be trapped there forever, Isaiah slowly flaying me to death with his belt.

Then a pair of lights erupted from overhead, through the broken ruins of the railing. Stacey and Juniper had twisted their flashlight irises to create the wide floodlight beams, and suddenly the dark stairwell was lit up like a stadium.

Isaiah and his belt were gone.

The door to the hallway slammed below me, as if someone had just fled the attic stairs.

Yeah, run away, Whippy, I thought. *Your time's almost up.*

Then I drew a deep breath and the pain came, erupting at every spot on my body that had slammed against the steps. Time seemed to speed up again, and I could hear Stacey and Juniper's voices clearly now.

"She's not talking! Why isn't she talking?" Juniper asked, shining her high-powered beam right into my face.

"Ellie!" Stacey shouted my name as she rounded the last cracked post of the railing and came down the stairs. Juniper copied her, and soon they were helping me sit up. "Are you hurt?" Stacey asked.

"I'll live," I said, but I was gritting my teeth in pain. A growing sense of anger began to displace my shock. Isaiah had just tried to kill me.

Stacey stood and pointed her flashlight at the landing. She walked down and checked the lower flight.

"I think he took off," I told her. The temperature had risen to its previous level already.

"We have to get him," Stacey said.

"We will." I looked at Juniper, who was pale and clearly terrified. "We can take care of it, Juniper. I promise. This is what we do."

She looked at me for a long time, as if thinking that over, and then she nodded.

I opened my hand, which still clutched the tiny model locomotive. The little iron smokestack and cowcatcher had gouged holes in my palm, drawing blood, as I'd crashed into the stairs. Not the most child-safe little toy.

As I stood, I slid the locomotive into my jeans pocket, and I started planning my ghost trap.

Chapter Twelve

I set up my air mattress at the intersection of the two upstairs halls. This gave me a view of the doors to the kids' rooms, plus the attic and master bedroom doors. Most importantly, it afforded a straight-on view of the door to the crafts room. My top priority was to keep the family safe from Isaiah if he emerged again.

As usual, I positioned the thermal and night cameras so I could see their display screens at a glance from where I sat. I added a motion detector in front of the door, too, with lights that would flicker if anything moved. I wanted to monitor that door as closely and in as many dimensions as possible.

Even closed, the door was a bluer hue on thermal than all the other doors in the hall, as if a deep freezer lay on the other side.

Stacey and I strapped on our microphone headsets so we could stay in touch, and we gave them a quick test. Juniper hung around, watching us.

"Good luck," Stacey said.

"Good luck seeing the ghost, or good luck not getting attacked again?" I asked.

"Both of those. You sure you don't want me to stay here with you?" Stacey asked.

"I'm sure I want you in the van watching the whole house."

"If you see him again, just scream."

"If *you* see him anywhere in the house, you'd better scream at me," I said.

"Done." Stacey smiled at Juniper. "Are you okay?"

"Yeah. A little freaked out." She glanced at the door to the attic, now tightly closed.

"You'll be fine. We're watching out for you." Stacey winked at her before leaving.

Juniper still didn't seem eager to go to bed—not surprising. It was a little past midnight, the rain was pounding outside, and she had just seen a ghost attack me in a potentially lethal way. Oh, and that small matter of a poltergeist tossing things around her room at night. The poor kid.

"Want to hang out?" I asked, since it was obvious she did. I sat down on my mattress, and she sat cross-legged on the hallway floor in front of me.

"Okay. So what do we do now?" she asked.

"We call this the observation period," I said. "We just soak up information about what's happening in the house. Tonight, it's kind of guard duty, too. We don't want Isaiah sneaking around causing trouble."

"How do we stop him if he comes back out?" Juniper glanced at the crafts room door, chewing her lip, then quickly looked away again, as if afraid staring at the door too long might cause it to open.

"Light is your first defense against ghosts." I gestured to the pair of tactical flashlights laid out in front of me, already pointing toward the crafts room door. "Ghosts don't like light. It doesn't hurt them, but it scrambles them and slows them down. Usually that's enough to send a ghost into hiding, unless it's really focused on doing something."

"Like trying to hurt you," Juniper said.

"Or some little task of their own. Ghosts kind of repeat the emotionally charged moments of their lives, their personal tragedies, again and again. Obsessive-compulsive. A lot of the time, they're lost in their memories and aren't even aware of the living people they're disturbing. Some of them have no idea they're even dead."

"What if the lights don't work?"

"Sound," I said, touching the little portable speaker on my belt.

"I've got a massive orchestral performance of Stravinsky's *Symphony of Psalms* ready to fire. The right kind of music is like hitting them with a big emotional blast that can drive them back."

"That's pretty cool. But what if that doesn't work?"

"I have a few other tricks up my sleeve," I said, though I really didn't have many. "Tonight I just want to keep Whippy McHalf-Face in his own room--"

Juniper laughed, and I realized I'd let slip the nickname Stacey and I had given Isaiah. We usually don't talk like that right in front of clients. Clients wouldn't necessarily like to hear us using silly nicknames for the dark things that torment them in their home. But sometimes you can't help it. I guess it helps you feel like you've got a handle on the monster you're facing.

"--and tomorrow, we'll try to trap him," I said.

"Okay. Sounds cool." Juniper looked around awkwardly for a minute, taking in my gear—flashlights, cameras, black toolbox containing those highly overrated "other tricks" of mine. Then she looked at me and smiled. "Hey, want me to read your fortune?"

"How would you do that?"

"Tarot. I'm pretty good at them. One time, I did it for Dayton and they said money was in his future, and then he found like twenty bucks in an old jacket. So that was kind of cool. I'll go get 'em!" Juniper rose to her feet.

I wouldn't have minded at all—anything to keep the girl calm and get her mind off the ghosts in her house—but I glanced at Toolie's door and remembered how the woman had told me not to encourage her daughter in the occult. I could imagine Toolie stepping out into the hall and finding me facing her daughter over a spread of major arcana.

Then I could imagine the Yelp review that would come afterward: "One star: Eckhart Investigations encouraged my daughter to practice black magic and worship Satan!"

"Thanks, but maybe not tonight," I said. "I'm kind of in the mood for avoiding the supernatural if possible."

"Okay." Juniper frowned, then smiled again. New idea. "Do you want some snacks?"

Actually, I did.

I accompanied Juniper down to the kitchen, notifying Stacey so she would keep a closer watch on the upstairs crafts room while I was away.

Juniper made us nachos from scratch—modern scratch, anyway. A bag of Tostitos, a bag of pre-shredded cheese, a jar of sliced jalapenos. My stomach was rumbling.

"What are you doing in there?" Stacey asked over my headphones. There weren't any cameras in the kitchen, since there hadn't been very much activity there. We'd stuck one night vision camera into the dining room where the pictures had fallen from the walls during a family argument, but nothing had happened there so far.

"We're making nachos," I told her.

"Oh, no fair!" I could hear her pout over my headphones, as clear as a bassoon. "I'm starving out here."

"We'll leave you a bowl by the kitchen door," I said. "When we're back in position, you can dash inside and grab it, then return to base."

"Aye aye, Roger," Stacey said. "'Base' just means the van, right?"

I sighed. "Jalapenos or not?"

"Jalapenos. And sour cream, if you got it?"

"Sour cream?" I asked Juniper. She nodded. Excellent.

When the nachos were done, we left the promised bowl sitting out for Stacey. It felt weirdly like leaving out cookies for Santa Claus.

"Hey, want to use my spirit board?" Juniper asked as we returned to the downstairs hall.

"No, never!" I said. "Those things are dangerous."

"Just asking. You don't have to get deranged about it."

"Have you ever used one in this house?" I asked.

"Yeah...kinda," she said. "With my boyfriend Dayton."

"How many times did you do it?"

"Mainly just once...or twice." She frowned and stopped walking. "Is this all my fault?"

"Definitely not all of it, but you might have stoked up the fire with that. What exactly happened?"

Juniper sighed. "It was Halloween. Dayton and me went out to the shed out back, you know, and lit some candles and stuff. To see if we could summon any spirits."

"What happened?"

"Nothing, we were just kind of fooling around." She blushed. "I mean, you know, playing around. Then it started to move, but it didn't really spell anything out. It just went in circles. Then we heard this banging on the door. And I screamed, I totally screamed. And

Dayton grabbed a lawn thingie, you know, a hoe, and he went to the door. I told him not to open it, but he did."

"What did you see?"

"Nothing. There was nobody around at all. That was the spooky thing. And then...stuff started happening around the house. The faucets turning on at night and everything. And my poltergeist." Her shoulders slumped as if a great boulder had just settled onto her back. "It *is* all my fault."

"It's not your fault the place is haunted," I said. "But promise me you won't play around with those things anymore, okay?"

She nodded.

"Seriously, promise," I said.

"I promise." She rolled her eyes just a little bit, then she smiled.

"How about a board game?" I pointed to the living room. "*Candy Land?*"

"That's a kid's game."

"It's okay to be a kid sometimes."

When we returned to the hall, armed with both nachos and a *Candy Land* set, I noticed a plinking sound, distinct from the rain hammering the roof and windows of the house.

"Oh, no," Juniper said.

I stepped past our thermal camera and looked into the powder room. The faucet was trickling, so I turned the water off. The metal handle felt like ice, burning my fingertips with cold.

"Stacey," I said, looking at the cameras. "This downstairs faucet turned itself on. Can you back up the footage and look for anomalies?"

"Okay, could take a minute," she replied over my headset.

"Make it fifty-nine seconds." I nodded at Juniper. "Let's head back upstairs."

We sat down at the crossroads of the two upstairs hallways again, and I tried not to think about the old folklore that says if you have business with the devil, you can meet him at any crossroads at midnight.

Juniper and I started our *Candy Land* game while the rain poured outside. *Candy Land* is kind of pointless—you draw cards that tell you where to move your little plastic-person token until somebody reaches the end. The main draw is the candy-themed scenery along the way. It was fun and silly enough to distract Juniper from her fears for the moment. We left a light on at the end of the kids' hall so we could see the game board.

"I found something," Stacey said over my headset.

"Go ahead," I told her.

"On thermal, I could see a little cloud of blue cold around the faucet just before it turned on. It drew back inside the faucet after the water started dripping. We also caught a couple of orbs on night vision."

"A couple? Do you think more than one entity was involved?" I could definitely imagine Noah and Luke turning on faucets at night as a prank.

"No idea," Stacey replied.

There wasn't much I could do with that information—we already knew *some* ghost was turning on the faucets at night—so I kept playing *Candy Land* with Juniper.

"Aw, licorice!" Juniper complained with a smile after moving her little yellow plastic guy onto one of the dreaded licorice spaces. "Lose a turn."

Then the lights went out. Juniper gasped in the darkness.

I immediately grabbed a flashlight and pushed my other one into Juniper's hands. I pointed mine right at the crafts room door.

Still closed.

The display screens of my cameras didn't show anything new—just the door, firmly in place. No new cold spots, no shadowy figures, not even the tiniest orb flitting past. The motion detector lay dark, not a single one of its tiny lights flickering.

"What happened?" Juniper whispered.

"It might just be the storm," I said, and then thunder rattled the house.

It sounded again a few seconds later, then a third time.

"There's no lightning," I whispered.

"Ellie, I'm picking up some loud bangs downstairs," Stacey said. "Are you hearing that?"

"I'll go check it out," I said, standing up. "Stay here, Juniper."

"Stay here by myself?" Juniper cast a worried look at the crafts room door.

"Okay, come with me, but stay close." I took her hand as we walked down the dark hallway, afraid something might grab her. She didn't protest at all, but instead clenched my hand tight in her own.

The loud boom sounded again as we descended the front stairs. I still hadn't seen any lightning.

We followed it to the kitchen. Something as pale as a dead fish smacked hard against the big window by the kitchen table.

"Wait here." I left Juniper standing by the counter while I approached the window. The pale, fleshy thing slapped the window again.

I pointed my flashlight through the window.

A white, transparent figure stood outside in the rain. I could just discern that it was a woman with pale, soaking wet hair clinging to her scalp and face. Some of her hair was buried under a kerchief, also soaking wet. She wore a heavy woolen dress with a high, lacy neck, also wet and plastered to her body in the rain. She was all blacks and whites, like a faded old photograph.

When she saw me—her eyes were hollow, twin windows to the rain-filled night beyond—her mouth opened wide as if screaming. I heard nothing.

She slapped the window again, harder this time, three quick blows, with that screaming look still frozen on her face.

A loud series of crashes sounded behind me.

I spun to see Juniper hunching forward, covering her ears. The row of cabinet doors above the counter behind her had opened all at once, by themselves. Dishes, glasses, and coffee mugs flew out and shattered on the kitchen floor, wave after wave of china and porcelain breaking on the tiles until the cabinets were entirely empty.

I grabbed Juniper and stood between her and the falling kitchenware, but the event was already over.

The girl was panting and shaking badly, and swaying on her feet as though suddenly exhausted.

"Is it over?" she whispered, rubbing her eyes. I turned to look at the window. The pale figure had vanished and ceased her banging.

"Maybe." I approached the window again, shining my light through it, but all I saw was rain, grass, and the swollen pond in the middle of the back yard.

"What in the name of Jesus Jones is going on down here?" Toolie swept into the room in a fuzzy green bathrobe and matching curlers. She took a sharp breath when she saw the destruction in the kitchen, then grabbed her daughter and looked her over. "Was anybody hurt?"

"We're okay," I said. "I need the two of you to stay right here."

"Where are you going?" Toolie asked. "Somebody needs to explain--"

"I'll be right back." I ran into the hall, unlocked the glass doors under the stairs, and ran out onto the patio, swinging my light everywhere. I was instantly drenched in cold rain.

She stood by the pond, watching me. She was still transparent, just barely visible, as though she wasn't strong enough to form a more complete apparition. She was dripping wet, which wasn't shocking in the rain, but ghosts aren't really affected by current physical weather. The *ghost* was soaking wet, as if she'd died by drowning.

"Catherine?" I asked, keeping my flashlight pointed at the ground so it wouldn't disturb her. I approached slowly across the grass. "Catherine Ridley?"

She opened her mouth in a silent scream, then pointed at me.

No. Not at me—past me, at something above my head.

I turned to look, but visibility was extremely poor, with the heavy rain and the rainclouds themselves blocking out the moon. I swept my flashlight across the house, trying to look into the upper windows.

There. My flashlight skimmed over it, and I brought it back for a closer look.

She wasn't pointing to a window, she was pointing to the roof.

A boy stood at the back corner of the roof, pale, soaked, and shivering. At first I guessed it was Noah or Luke, but the boy seemed solid, not a fragile-frost apparition like Catherine by the pond. An attic dormer window was wide open, several feet above and behind him.

"Crane?" I shouted. "Crane, is that you?"

I dropped my flashlight beam down and to one side of him, because I didn't want to risk the glare blinding him into a misstep. He was already right at the edge, the very corner of the roof, with a twenty-five foot drop to a brick patio below. His toes had to be in the rain gutter already.

"Crane, don't move!" I shouted. What was the kid doing up there? My heart raced in fear—if he fell, there was a good chance he would die.

"Ellie, what's happening?" Stacey's voice crackled.

"Stacey, go into the kitchen and get Toolie," I said. "Right now. Crane's on the roof and he might fall."

"Holy cow!"

The van was parked in the driveway, on the far side of the back yard from where I stood. Stacey leaped out and raced to the back door I'd just left.

On the roof above, Crane stood silently. He'd done nothing to acknowledge my presence, as if he were sleepwalking.

"Crane!" I said. "Listen to me carefully. You need to sit down right where you are. Don't move."

"Leave me alone!" Crane shouted back. Right, like I was just going to wander off and make some popcorn while he stood on the brink of death.

Stacey, Toolie, and Juniper ran out from the glass doors, sloshing through puddles as they crossed the patio toward me.

"Where is he?" Toolie asked, squinting up at the roof through the rain.

Juniper pointed her flashlight right at Crane, and he swayed a little. I grabbed her flashlight and changed its angle.

"Don't blind him," I told her.

"What do I do? What do I do?" Juniper asked.

"You and Stacey stay right here, keep talking to him!" I said, shouting to be heard over the ever-growing downpour. I grabbed Toolie by the shoulder. "Follow me!" I shouted.

I turned and ran for the door, not waiting for a response. Toolie was kind of husky and probably wouldn't be able to keep up with me, anyway.

I ran through the kitchen, down the hall, and up the stairs, leaving behind muddy bootprints. Each second felt like an hour, and I was certain Crane had already slipped and fallen, that I was already too late.

The upstairs hallway also seemed to take far, far too long to traverse. I bolted up the attic stairs, past the spot where I'd fallen and gained some nasty bruises earlier that night. I stumbled over debris from the broken railing.

As luck would have it, I then had to run all the way to the far side of the attic to reach the open dormer window. Rain slanted in through it, collecting in a puddle on the attic floorboards.

The window sill was at shoulder height for me—how the heck had the kid managed to get up there? I had to find a sturdy wooden chest and drag it over. I might have been able to do a pull-up and heaved myself over the sill, but it was slippery, and so was the steep roof outside. I didn't want to slip and die if I could avoid it.

I placed one foot on the chest. As I brought up my other foot, the entire chest slid sideways and slammed into a roof support post. I lost my balance and toppled to the floorboards, banging my elbow so hard that my left forearm turned numb and tingly.

I thought the chest had simply slipped in the water beneath it, but then I heard the laughter of an unseen child in the air nearby.

"Stop!" I shouted, pushing myself to my feet.

"You stop," a childish voice whispered back at me.

I didn't have time for this kindergarten-level debate. I shoved the chest back into place, clambered on top of it and up onto the windowsill.

The pitched roof below did not look welcoming. A sheen of water ran down it, turning it into a slick ramp that would take me straight into oblivion. The rain was still falling hard and heavy.

I eased my leg out into the rain. My calf boots weren't the worst things I could have been wearing, I guess, but I would've traded them for cleats in a second. Or those clawed shoes worn by the guys who work way up in the tree tops. Yep, a pair of those would've been great.

I climbed out legs first and stayed on my hands and knees, since it seemed less likely I'd break my neck that way.

"Crane!" I called out, not too loudly, because I didn't want to startle him. I crawled slowly toward the boy, feeling like I'd slip and fall any second. Maybe charging onto the roof after the kid wasn't the best plan, but it was all I had.

He turned to look at me, and that was when I saw the shape standing beside him on the roof.

The figure was made entirely of a strange hollow space where no raindrops fell, like the Invisible Man standing out in the rain. This looked more like a boy than a man, just a little taller than Crane himself. Noah or Luke, I assumed—whichever one hadn't been hanging around in the attic, waiting to shove the chest out from beneath me.

If the ghosts could push that heavy chest, then they could push me, and it wouldn't take much to send me sliding down over the edge.

"Crane, back away from there," I said, still inching my way toward him.

"But they'll call me a chicken," Crane said.

"Who?"

"Noah and Luke. They dared me to do it."

"Crane, you're in a dangerous place right now. You could die," I said.

"They said it doesn't hurt that much." He looked down at the patio below, maybe at his sister, who was shouting at him to back up and go inside.

I had a hard time swallowing while I digested what he'd just said.

"You mean Noah and Luke want you to die?" I asked.

"So I can be like them." Crane nodded.

"You can't do that, Crane." I was easing closer and closer on my hands and knees across the roof, but I didn't want to rush. I could have startled him, or lost my footing. "You still have a long life ahead. And your family will miss you."

Crane looked at the invisible boy-shape in the rain beside him, as though listening.

"I'll still be in the house," Crane said. "I'll just be a ghost."

"That's not the same. And remember, your family can't see and hear ghosts like you can. They'll barely know you're there." This was cutting into my heart a little, trying to talk a seven-year-old boy down from suicide. "Believe me, you don't want to die, Crane."

The boy-shape in the rain beside him turned toward me.

Then it charged.

It became an odd roundish shape, like an elongated ball, as it flew at me through the sheets of rain. I didn't have time to grab my flashlight from my holster. I didn't have time to do anything except try to tighten my grip on the slick shingles, the rainwater coursing around my fingertips in a rushing creek.

The thing struck me hard, striking me like a bowling ball launched from a catapult. I toppled and slid down the steep roof, my arms and then my head going right over the edge.

Stacey turned her flashlight on me, shouting my name, and Juniper pointed.

The bricks far below shimmered in the light from the kitchen windows, coated in a sheen of water that would do nothing to soften my face-first impact against the patio.

I grabbed onto the overflowing gutter and felt it creak under me. I tried to dig my toes into the shingles. I'm not sure if that helped, but I'd stopped sliding, and my skull had not bashed open on the hard red surface below.

I looked over at Crane, who remained right at the corner of the roof, staring at me. He looked scared now, where before he'd had more of a distant, hypnotized look on his face.

"It's okay," I said. "Don't move."

I pulled myself back from the edge and crawled toward him. I held out my hand.

"Come on, Crane," I said. "Come inside with me."

He glanced from me to the bricks below, as if indecisive now. I looked out for the ghostly boy-shape in the rain, but I couldn't find where he was. Not exactly comforting.

"Crane!" his mother's voice shouted. Toolie had finally made it up the stairs and to the attic window. I wondered if the other boy-ghost had delayed her somehow, or maybe she'd been there shouting the whole time, but the high winds had eaten up her voice.

He turned his head at the sound of Toolie shouting for him. Now he looked flat-out terrified, not indecisive at all, as if the craziness of what he'd done was finally sinking in.

"Come on, Crane," I said. "Take my hand."

The boy slowly reached out to me. His fingers were cold.

I helped him to his hands and knees and pointed him back to the open window. Then I crawled along behind him. If he slipped, I would either stop him from falling, or I would cushion him when we slammed into the bricks below. Too bad there was nobody to cushion me—that was one major flaw in my idea.

He inched his way up the roof. I was tense, waiting for one of the boy ghosts to strike at him, or at me.

Crane made it up the window, though, and Toolie grabbed him as soon as he was in reach. She grunted as she lifted him inside.

I crawled in after them, easing my feet down onto the chest, watching the shadows suspiciously.

Toolie was shouting at Crane, who cringed, and then she hugged him.

Outside the window, two hollow boy-shapes stood in the rain, watching me. Noah and Luke might have been children when they'd died, but we couldn't afford to think of them as benign, mischievous little Caspers anymore.

They had tried to convince Crane to kill himself. They were now the enemy.

I closed the window and latched it shut, and the boy-shapes vanished.

Chapter Thirteen

A little while later, Stacey and I sat in the living room along with the entire family—the excessive clutter of furniture meant everybody had comfortable seating.

Toolie had made Crane change his clothes, and now he sat beside her on an antique Edwardian chaise while she dried his hair with a SpongeBob towel. Gord watched his son from a nearby chair, clearly worried. Juniper drowsed in one of the high-backed chairs, looking drained.

"I still don't understand why you'd go up there," Toolie said to Crane. "Have you lost your mind?"

"They said it would be okay," Crane whispered.

"Who said?" Gord asked his son. "Your invisible...friends?"

Crane shrugged. "They're not invisible to me."

"Crane, those boys are not your friends," I said. "Nobody who wants you to die is your friend. That's a good general rule of thumb in life."

"They just want me to be with them," Crane said. "They want me to help them."

"Help them with what?" I asked.

Crane fell silent.

"Answer her, Crane," Toolie said. "I mean it."

"Just help them," he whispered. "They don't want me to talk about it."

"I don't give two saltines and a bowl of soup what they want," Toolie said. "Promise me you'll never do *anything* like that again, Crane. Promise me." She turned his head to make him look her in the eyes.

"Okay," he said, but there wasn't a lot of conviction.

"Can you tell me anything else?" I asked Crane.

He shook his head.

"Would it be okay if Juniper took him into the library for a minute?" I asked Toolie.

"All right." She sighed. "You keep an eye on him, Junie. Junie?"

Stacey reached over and shook the girl awake.

"Huh?" Juniper looked around, blinking. "What did I miss?"

"Take Crane into the library and watch him," Toolie said.

"Oh." Juniper rubbed her eyes. "Yep. Come on, Crane, let's find a book to read." Juniper took her brother's hand, gently escorted him to the next room, and slid the door closed.

"What do we do?" Toolie asked.

"First, someone needs to be with Crane at all times," I said.

"Obviously." She nodded. "Do we take him to a...therapist or something?"

"Calvin knows somebody who's sympathetic to ghost stories," I said. I didn't mention that I'd gone to the same person for therapy when I was younger, on Calvin's advice. "Also, we have a friend who's a psychic and consults on our cases. He might understand Crane's situation better than any of us could. He might be able to speak with him."

"Oh, yeah, Jacob would be great at that," Stacey said, flashing a smile that was a little too wide for the situation.

"I was going to call him in for a look around, anyway," I said. "We're still trying to piece together the full situation here. I think we should definitely go ahead with our plans to trap Isaiah tomorrow night."

"What about the two boys?" Toolie said. "They need to go. Right now."

"They're trapped in a drama with the ghost of their father," I said. "It's very likely that Isaiah's presence is keeping them here. If we get rid of him, the boys might leave on their own."

"What if they...don't?" Gord asked.

"Then we'll trap them, too," I said. "I should mention that I also encountered another ghost."

"Oh, goodness' sake," Toolie said.

"I believe it was Catherine, Isaiah's wife, the mother of Noah and Luke," I said. "I recommend we not take any action to remove her at this point."

"Why not?" Gord asked.

"Because she's the one who alerted us about Crane tonight," I said. "I think she was banging on the window to tell us. Then I saw her outside by the pond...I mean, in your back yard...and she pointed him out to me. She saved his life."

Gord and Toolie looked at each other.

"Well," Toolie finally said. "It's good to feel like one of them's on our side in this thing, at least. Now if we could just get rid of the others."

"We will," I told her. "We won't stop until this house is safe for your children again."

Chapter Fourteen

Stacey and I left the house right at daybreak, exhausted. On my way home, I forced myself to take a detour by the Historical Association mansion. Grant had left me a package on the back porch, a manuscript box filled with photocopied letters and other documents surrounding the Ridley family. Fortunately, no document burglars had stolen it during the night.

I went home and crashed.

When my alarm woke me at one, I took my time making breakfast—a banana, a hard-boiled egg, some jelly I pretty much ate off a spoon. I was moving slowly and stiffly thanks to old Whippy throwing me down the attic stairs. Son of Whippy had done a number on me as well, slamming me hard against the roof. I was starting to hate that whole undead family.

I did a little bit of yoga stretching, keeping to the easy stuff like sun salutations, but I still winced each time I changed poses. Then I ran a bath and climbed in with a sheaf of the papers Grant had prepared for me.

Catherine's letters were much harder to read without the big magnifying glass, but I managed to dig my way through them, taking in all the stuff I hadn't read yet. Catherine tried to put up a good front, but there were multiple asides about Isaiah's "rough discipline" approach to the boys.

I got the sense that Catherine might have been a little abused, too, from lines like: "Isaiah is strict enough with Eliza and me when we step out of line, but he reserves his worst for the boys." Or a few comments like: "Some days I feel so dark, I wish the earth would open and swallow me whole."

A couple of weeks after Isaiah's death, when the family began to experience the haunting, there was a reference to "just when we'd thought the darkness had lifted," a strange sentiment for a woman whose husband had just died.

And she felt a great deal of guilt about the ghost tormenting the family and wrecking the home.

I began to wonder. Isaiah wielded his horrible belt-whip with his right hand, but the bullet hole I'd seen was in the *left* side of his head. If he was right-handed, wouldn't he have been more likely to shoot himself in the right temple?

It was hardly solid evidence, but it indicated another possibility. Maybe he hadn't committed suicide. Maybe he'd been murdered, and the gun placed in his hand afterward. The state of forensics in the eighteen-fifties had been nonexistent, making suicide much easier to fake.

What if he'd been murdered? Catherine might have grown fed up with his abuse, with watching him lash his belt across her children, and decided to kill him. Or maybe there was some third party I didn't know about, something to do with his business or political interests.

I flagged those ideas for later consideration and continued reading.

I sat up when I discovered the coroner's reports, which Grant had tracked down and helpfully included.

Isaiah was declared a suicide, shot through the left temple, just as I'd observed when I saw his ghost.

Catherine, Noah, and Luke had drowned in the pond out back.

Eliza, however, had *not* drowned. She'd been found inside the house, in a cabinet in the upstairs office, with abrasions all over her throat. The death certificate had given the cause of death as "asphyxiation," just like her mother and two brothers. It hadn't specified that she'd been asphyxiated in an entirely different manner.

That new information hit me like a mini-bombshell, altering my already vague and confused picture of what had really happened to the family.

The coroner had concluded that Catherine had first strangled her daughter, then drowned herself and her sons in the pond. This struck me as a little doubtful—Noah had been twelve years old. Unless he'd been particularly sick or weak, it seemed like it would be difficult for an average woman to hold him underwater until he died. Maybe he had been sickly. I had no way of knowing.

It was beyond macabre to imagine Catherine doing all of that, including forcing herself to stay underwater until she drowned.

"Why would she have done it?" I whispered. My cat, lying on the fuzzy bathroom mat, turned his patchy black-and-white head to look at me. "That doesn't make any sense, Bandit. If she killed her husband to protect the children, why would she kill the children?"

Bandit lost interest and looked away, deciding the tag at the edge of the mat was more interesting. He idly pawed at it.

"Maybe she didn't kill her husband, then," I said. "Maybe she thought it was suicide. Maybe it really *was* suicide. Still—why the daughter first, then everyone else dies in a different way?"

Bandit rolled to his feet, approached the tub, then rose up and put his front paws on the edge of the bath. For a second, it looked like he was actually going to say something. Then he lowered his head and began lapping up bath water.

"That's the last time I call you in for a homicide consultation," I told my cat. He didn't even glance at me.

After my bath, as I was drying off, my Aunt Clarice called from Virginia. I'd lived with her from the time my parents died when I was fifteen until I moved back to Savannah for college.

She told me about some gossip from her bridge club, and some gossip from a ladies' group at church, and I pretended to be really interested. She was just calling to talk. The more I encouraged her to talk, the fewer questions she would end up asking me.

The questions were usually the same: was I still doing that same sort of work (asked with distaste)? Had I met a nice young man yet, and when were the babies due? I wasn't getting any younger and definitely didn't want to end up a useless old maid at the age of thirty. Well, not in so many words, but that was what she meant.

She was mainly just checking to see if I was okay, living alone "in that big city." Right. I assured her I was, and avoided mentioning how two different ghosts had nearly killed me in the past twenty-four hours. No reason to worry her.

With my family duties squared away for the week, I got ready for work and headed to the office.

While I loaded a few traps into the special rack built into the back corner of the van, Calvin dropped down in his elevator cage from his apartment on the upper floor. His bloodhound Hunter jogged out, wagged his tail at me, and stopped at my feet for some petting.

"Trap time?" Calvin asked.

"Yep." I caught him up to date on the case. "It looks like you were right about our missing ghosts. Catherine definitely made an appearance."

"And the little girl?" he asked.

"No sign of her yet," I said. "Maybe that's something Jacob can find out about."

"You're really softening on the issue of psychic consultants, aren't you?" he asked.

"I'm softening on the subject of Jacob, at least. He was a big help last time."

"But you're not softening on that subject as much as Stacey," he added, with a little smile. "Should I make us sandwiches?"

"No, thanks," I said. Calvin usually buys those ultra-discount deli meats, the ones that stick out because of their unnatural color. "Can I have a dime?" I walked over to an old metal card catalog we'd salvaged from a local library. A ring thick with keys hung on a nail in the wall beside it.

"What decade?" Calvin asked.

"Eighteen-forties, eighteen-fifties." I sifted through the keys until I found the one I needed, and then I unlocked one of the rows of miniature metal doors. I slid out the drawer. Instead of index cards, it had little Tupperware containers, labeled by decade. I picked up one holding coins from the eighteen-fifties.

Since money can be one of a person's obsessions in life, a certain number of ghosts are still attracted to it after death. Unfortunately, we deal with a lot of ghosts from past centuries, and they don't really respond to coins made of tin and zinc.

Calvin collects old silver coins, searching the internet for the most worn, chipped, and dented ones, those barely worth more than melt value. They can come in handy.

I lucked out and found one dated 1851. It was a Seated Liberty, a very common design, the goddess Liberty with stars and a shield.

The goddess's image had been worn down and tarnished until she was little more than a shadow.

The coin had been struck the same year Isaiah had died. Its deteriorated condition made it seem even more like suitable money for the dead.

"In mint condition, that would be worth eight hundred dollars today," Calvin said.

"What's this one worth?"

"About fifteen bucks."

"We might have to bury this one," I said. "Isaiah seems a little vicious. With, you know, the studded torture belt and trying to kill me and everything." When we remove a not-particularly-dangerous ghost from a house, we do a catch-and-release. A walled cemetery in a ghost town makes an ideal wildlife refuge for ghosts, and we know where several of those are.

With the more dangerous ghosts, though, the violent and hostile ones, we never release them from the trap. We bury the trap with the ghost inside, which means we bury the bait inside the trap, too. That's why we use cheap junk silver instead of shiny gold, even though gold might be more alluring and effective bait. You don't want to bill the clients for a coin worth hundreds of dollars if you can avoid it.

"Do you have *any* thoughts about what might have happened in that house?" I asked Calvin. "To me, the only scenario that makes sense is the obvious. Isaiah lost his money and killed himself, and then his widow, crazy with grief, kills her three kids and herself."

"But you don't believe that one," he said. "Or you wouldn't have a problem with it."

"Catherine saved our clients' little boy, Crane," I said. "He might have died without her."

"Perhaps she's trying to atone for her sins in life," Calvin said.

"Maybe."

"What's a scenario that makes less sense?" Calvin asked me.

"One where Catherine kills her husband *and* her kids. The only motive for killing her husband was to save the kids from him. And why strangle the little girl upstairs, separate from the rest?" I asked.

"Perhaps Eliza's death was more of an impulse, and the death of the boys required more planning," Calvin said.

"And where does Eliza's poltergeist fit into it?" I asked. "Between her father's death and his ghost haunting the house, I could see how she might be stressed enough to create one, if she had the psychic ability to do it."

"I suppose the poltergeist might have increased the stress on the mother," he said. "She would have figured it was her dead husband harassing the household."

"Which it might have been, but it was more consistent with poltergeist activity focused on Eliza," I said. "It even happened during the day, all over the house, wherever Eliza was. That's more like a poltergeist than a revenant like Isaiah. Ghosts are mostly nocturnal..."

Calvin nodded.

"But I still don't think Catherine did it," I said. "I saw her. She didn't seem malevolent. I just didn't get that feeling from her."

"Aren't you always telling Stacey that we should act on observable evidence and logic, and not our feelings?" Calvin asked me with a little smile.

"Yeah. True. Speaking of putting feelings ahead of logic, I could really go for a pizza right now."

"You sure you don't want a bologna sandwich instead?"

"Pretty sure, but thanks for asking."

We ordered the pizza, and it arrived about the time Stacey did. She was finally, reluctantly, learning to dress in a way that was less likely to get her scratched or bitten by a hostile ghost. Tonight it was canvas pants and a long-sleeved, high-collared shirt.

Stacey and I loaded the big stamper, the device that slams the lid down onto the trap at high speed, into the van. With the heavy lifting done, we sat down and ate.

Mushrooms and garlic. Crunchy, buttery crust. Yum.

Then we were off to work.

On the way to the Paulding house, we caught a view of low black thunderheads spitting lightning into the ocean. According to the Weather Channel, we could expect another dark and stormy night in the ghost-infested old mansion. Hooray.

Chapter Fifteen

We arrived at our clients' well before dark, because we wanted to set the trap before the sun went down.

Gord and Crane were in the kitchen, watching *Pokemon* on a digital tablet. Toolie was home from work, making some kind of chicken and broccoli casserole in the kitchen. Juniper came downstairs soon after we arrived to see what was happening. The family seemed like they were trying to act normally, maybe for Crane's sake, but Juniper and her parents were clearly uneasy and nervous under their forced smiles.

I noticed they kept flashlights and electric lanterns near them now, to help defend against any ghost attacks. Assorted religious items had been set out in the family room—a cross, a print of Jesus standing in the dark with his hands glowing, an old Bible, and a Christmas Nativity scene on the coffee table—as if to ward off evil spirits.

If I did my job right, those spirits would soon be gone. The most dangerous one, anyway.

Clients usually have a few questions about the ghost traps, and I don't generally like explaining them in the house where the ghost might hear, so after a few minutes I led Toolie, Juniper, and Crane outside to the van.

"Here's the basic trap," I said, lifting a two-foot-high hard plastic cylinder from the back of the van. I explained it quickly: the innermost layer was a jar of thick, heavily leaded glass, very difficult for ghosts to penetrate, impossible for most. The second layer was copper mesh electrified by a battery pack concealed at the bottom—this created an electromagnetic cage for the ghost. The outer layer was just clear, hard plastic to insulate the wiring.

"What do you do with ghosts after you trap them?" Crane asked. It was the first thing he'd said since we'd arrived.

"It depends on the ghost," I said. "If they're not dangerous and don't hurt people, we can release them into a special kind of sanctuary, an old graveyard where they can wander free within the walls. If they are dangerous, we bury the trap so they can't bother anyone else."

Crane seemed to think this over a minute, then he nodded.

"We bait the trap with candles to draw them inside, because ghosts can feed on the heat," I said. I pulled the little Ziploc baggie of ghost-bait from my pocket. "We also have some special bait for Isaiah. Here's a little train toy, a promotional item from his business that failed. And here's a silver dime from the year he died, since he was so worried about money. These other two items are a couple of cufflinks Stacey found in the attic, which we think belonged to him."

"So he's not going to haunt our house anymore?" Crane asked. "You'll make the bad one go away?"

"That's right," I told him.

Without another word, Crane turned and walked inside. Maybe it hadn't been such a good idea to explain the trap to him. He was in direct contact with the ghosts, and I didn't want him spilling the beans to Noah and Luke, in case the spilled beans would then somehow pass to Isaiah himself, warning him away from the trap.

"Don't tell any of the ghosts what I just showed you," I called after Crane while he approached the back door to his house. He glanced back over his shoulder, but didn't say anything before walking inside.

Juniper helped us carry some of the gear upstairs to the crafts room—as I instructed, we didn't say a word while inside the cold, unpleasant-feeling room. Stacey and I carried the big stamper upstairs. We set up the cumbersome, four-foot-high structure in the middle of the room, not far from the sewing machine. The stamper is a pneumatic device that sends the lid of the ghost trap down at high speed, sealing the top before the ghost has a chance to sneak back out. Usually.

We set it up in silence, with the same heavy feeling of something watching us from the cold shadows of the room. I slid the trap into place and checked my remote. The little liquid-crystal display screen on the remote told me the temperature and EMF reading inside the trap. They matched the rest of the room—inexplicably cool, about ten degrees lower than the rest of the house, with high electromagnetic readings. No surprises there.

Stacey checked the thermal and night vision cameras, which now pointed directly at the trap. Everything was ready to go. The bait was still in my pocket. I would save that for the last minute, when we were finally ready to light the trap, then sit and watch it for hours.

Stacey and I shivered as we left the room and closed the door. Juniper had watched silently from the hall.

"Okay," I said, feeling relieved. "Let's go make our rounds."

We checked the cameras and microphones all over the house. Jacob arrived at sunset—Stacey almost bolted to the door when the doorbell rang, but she slowed down and let Juniper open it.

"Hey, are you the psychic?" Juniper asked.

"Are you the one with the ghost problem?" Jacob gave her a half-smile. He wore his black retro-framed glasses and a white button-up shirt of the type that normally goes with a coat and tie. Some mildly distressed skinny jeans, new sneakers.

"Hey, come on, Jacob!" Stacey hurried forward and took his arm. "You're late. Almost."

"Almost late? Doesn't that mean I'm exactly on time?" he asked, allowing himself to be towed into the house.

"Do we show him where the ghosts are?" Juniper asked.

"No, remember, we don't tell him anything," I said. "We let him walk around and see what he finds."

We introduced Jacob to the rest of the family—well, Stacey handled the introductions, staying fairly close to him. The Pauldings were sitting down for a late dinner, the table set with paper plates and mismatched plastic cups.

When Jacob and Crane looked at each other, I could almost feel something click in the air between them. Psychics. I guess it takes one to know one. I imagined them sending rapid telepathic messages to each other, though I doubt that was actually happening.

"Juniper, take your seat," Toolie said.

"Can't I hang out with them?" Juniper asked, pointing to me.

"Sit down and eat your casserole!" Toolie said, and Juniper huffed and sank into her chair.

"Okay, show me around," Jacob said.

"This way." Stacey took his arm and led him out of the room. As he left, Jacob gave Crane a quick nod. That was all the communication that had passed between them, as far as I could tell, but Crane stared at Jacob with intense interest while we left to explore the house.

I felt impatient as we walked around the first floor, Jacob pausing here and there.

"I'm feeling some residual stuff down here, but nothing huge," he said, and that was the gist of his comments until we walked upstairs.

"That kid has something, doesn't he?" Jacob asked in a low voice, now that we were farther away from the family.

"Like what?" I asked, cutting off Stacey's obvious rush to agree with him.

"He has some ability," Jacob said.

"Way to be vague, Jacob," Stacey told him with a little grin. "Do you mean juggling ability? Ventriloquism? Playing the violin?"

"He's probably the one who's seen the ghosts more than anyone else," Jacob said. Stacey smiled and nodded.

"Let's keep moving," I said.

I can't say Jacob had any huge revelations for us inside the house, but what he found did fit with what we already knew.

In Juniper's room: "Yeah, there's something in here," he said. He kept looking up at the corners of the room. "It's not exactly a spirit, not exactly a dead person. It's something else. Demonic, maybe?" He shook his head. "I don't know. I don't think it's human."

It sounded to me like he was picking up on the poltergeist.

In Crane's room: "A lot of stuff happening here, in and out, but I don't sense anything *dwelling* here, if that makes sense."

"It totally does," Stacey said. I cut her a look to be quiet—we didn't want to confirm or deny anything, because that could interfere with his own clarity. I'm skeptical about psychics, anyway. I know some people do have ability, and Jacob is clearly one of them, but you still don't want to lead them with too much information.

In Toolie's room: "The woman living here is very troubled, I think."

He didn't find much in the lesser-used rooms of the second floor, including two spare bedrooms connected by a bathroom hung with bright decorative towels embroidered with puffy flowers. It was a guest bathroom, with a scented candle and a basket of colorful soap balls, but no actual personal items like toothbrushes or make-up. No activity reported here, either by the family or by Jacob.

When we reached the crafts room, though, he had an obvious reaction. Of course, the trap sitting in the middle of it might have been a clue.

We hadn't yet lit the candles inside the trap to attract the ghosts. Ghosts tend to be most active in the darkest and quietest hours of the night, from about midnight to four a.m. Each one is different, though, and there are ghosts who appear during the daytime, as well as ghosts who pop out at full steam the moment the sun goes down.

Jacob took one and a half steps into the crafts room and froze. It's kind of funny when he does that, like those pointer dogs that go completely still, using their whole body as an arrow to indicate where the prey was hiding.

"Well?" I asked.

"You don't need me to tell you this room is a bad place," he said, his voice low. "Ugh. I can feel it everywhere. This thing...this male thing that used to be human, a long time ago. His presence just fills the room like smoke. I think he died here. Violently."

Stacey shuddered and moved closer to Jacob, touching his hand. Using fear as a cover to flirt with him, I'm pretty sure.

"Is he dangerous?" she whispered, looking into Jacob's eyes. Overdoing it. I mean, come on, she'd been in scarier situations than this.

"I think he is," Jacob replied. He was gazing right back into her eyes.

"If you could both quit moon-goggling each other for a second, I'd like some more specific details from Jacob," I said.

"Yeah, sorry." He let go of Stacey's hand and looked around. "Very cold in here, and I mean that in every possible way. Okay. I think this ghost kind of goes out and patrols the house a little bit, very late at night. He's looking for troublemakers. He wants to punish them. He has some kind of weapon he carries. He's angry, and he takes it out on the others..."

"The others?" I asked.

"The other ghosts. There must be more in this house, or at least he thinks there are, because he hunts them. He..." Jacob stopped and his eyes widened. "He knows I'm here. Unless you want to fight him now, we should maybe..." He backed toward the door, pulling Stacey along with him.

I couldn't see anything unusual in the room, aside from the heavy shadows, but I could definitely feel Isaiah watching me. For a second, I could smell him, too—wet earth and rotten leather.

"Let's go," I whispered.

I wasn't looking forward to my inevitable return visit to this room, to bait and light the trap. The little bits of bait remained in my pocket. I didn't want Whippy to see them just yet.

We closed the crafts room door firmly behind us as we returned to the warmer, brighter hallway.

"I assume that guy's the problem," he told Stacey, pointing to the room we'd just left.

"He's a real monster," Stacey agreed. "Ready to see what's behind door number three?"

She opened the attic door, and he leaned through the doorframe and looked up the stairs.

"Oh, yeah," he said. "We're not done yet."

We flipped on the attic lights—two bulbs came to life, but the one above our heads stayed dark. Stacey and I drew our flashlights from their holsters as we accompanied Jacob up the stairs.

We'd cleaned up the splintered chunks of broken railing, just as we'd helped clean up the thousands of glass and china fragments in the kitchen. Jacob eyed the upright remnants of the railing as he passed around them.

"Watch your step," he said.

"You have no idea," Stacey whispered.

He was quiet for a minute, looking around the heaps of old decorations, boxes, and toys.

"Don't mind me," he murmured. Maybe he was talking to the creepy life-size Santa Claus lying under the plastic tree hung with tinsel.

He advanced deeper into the attic, ducking under the low beams.

"A lot of energy up here," he said, a little louder. "More than one. They feel young, male. They're kind of mischievous, but they're also turning dark. Tortured souls. They're always running and hiding from the other guy, the one on the second floor. They hide up here.

So many hiding places..." Jacob removed his glasses and squinted at a shadow melting across the wall in the moving glow of my flashlight. "Yeah. The other one, the bad one, he sees these two boys as his property, somehow. Slaves, maybe?" Jacob frowned.

"What do they want?" I asked.

"They want to get rid of him," Jacob said. "That's pretty clear to me. End his nightly hunts, how he beats them when he catches them playing. But they're not strong enough to do it. They want help."

"What kind of help?" I asked. It reminded me of what Crane had said, of course, about them wanting his help, wanting him to become a ghost like them.

"To free themselves from him, to finally overthrow his rule of the house," Jacob said. "Strength in numbers. That's what they're thinking. Strength in numbers." He shrugged. "That's all I'm getting from them. They aren't very open with me. They want us out of here. They don't like for the living to come into the attic at all, because it could draw his attention up here, into their hiding place. I guess he normally avoids coming up here...he patrols the rest of the house, but the attic's like his blind spot. It must be." He nodded. "They want us to leave right now."

"Ask them how they died," I said.

"Okay. How did...?" He looked off toward the far end of the attic, where we'd found a few of the Ridley family possessions.

A creaky, rusty sound echoed from the direction.

Stacey and I pointed our flashlights toward it. She stepped in front of Jacob, as if ready to protect him from any dangerous spirits.

Our lights found the heap of old toys near the back. The rusty, spring-mounted rocking horse nodded up and down, just slightly, the springs screeching with each little movement.

My heart beat a little faster, and I was ready to escape down the attic steps. Not that those had offered me much such safety in the past.

"Noah! Luke!" I snapped, trying to sound as tough and firm as I could manage. I widened the iris of my flashlight and swept it back and forth, chasing away flickering shadows. "Stay away from us!"

"Wow, they hate you," Jacob told me. "They look angry now. You can really see their dark and tormented side now."

"I'd rather not see that if we can avoid it," I said.

"What about me?" Stacey asked. "Do they hate me?"

"They've barely noticed you're here," Jacob assured her. "They aren't paying any attention to you, don't worry."

"Oh." She frowned a little, as if slightly disappointed.

"How did they die?" I asked again.

"Choking," Jacob said. "No, wait. I'm seeing water. Drowning, maybe. It was violent, not accidental. Somebody killed them."

"Who?" I asked.

"Now they won't tell me. They're retreating." Jacob shook his head. "That's all they're going to say to me right now. They want us out of here."

"Good enough for now, I suppose," I said. Jacob hadn't told us much that was new. I was eager to get him out of the house. By which I mean into the back yard, around the pond area.

"I think he's doing great," Stacey said, with a smile for Jacob.

I turned away and rolled my eyes just a little as I led the way down the attic stairs.

We walked out into a drizzling rain—nothing too heavy, but I knew there was a lot more on the way.

Jacob wandered in a slow circle around the pond, keeping clear of the marshy mud at the edges. Stacey and I stood back, letting him do his thing.

"There's a woman here," Jacob said as he returned toward us, looking into the water. "She's confused, she's trapped somehow." He cocked his head as if listening. Stacey watched him with a little bit of awe, still fascinated by his abilities. "She's trying to get inside the house, but she can't. She's worried about her children. They're stuck inside the house with the bad one...I think the ghosts in the attic are her children. She knows he's treating them badly, attacking and abusing them. She'd do anything to stop him. Even kill him." He shook his head. "Well, that doesn't make a lot of sense. They're already dead, but...that's how she feels, I guess."

"*Did* she kill him?" I asked.

Jacob hesitated for a minute, then nodded. "It's possible. I wouldn't be surprised. She's pretty confused, like I said. I think her death came as a shock, and she never really got over it."

"How did she die?" Stacey asked.

"Drowning." He nodded at the pond. "Just like the two up in the attic. They all drowned right here."

"How exactly did they drown?" I asked.

"I believe their lungs filled with water and they died," Jacob said, lifting an eyebrow. "That's how it usually goes."

"I'm not joking," I said. "Did she kill herself?"

"Oh! No, no. Somebody held her underwater. She died struggling and kicking."

"Who did it?" I asked. My heart skipped a little. I really needed that answer.

Jacob closed his eyes. A few expressions crossed his face—something like confusion melting into frustration and then horror.

"She doesn't know," he finally said.

"How could she not know?" Stacey asked.

"She didn't see anything. She was out here with her boys, gathering logs from the firewood heap there..." Jacob, his eyes still closed, pointed to a flower bed that featured no firewood at all. "It was cold, so cold, definitely winter. Then they were all in the pond, being held down, choking on water that was almost freezing." He shivered and wrapped his arms around himself.

"All three at the same time?" I asked.

"She never saw what killed them," Jacob said, his voice low. He finally opened his eyes. "It was like something invisible."

"Like a ghost?" Stacey suggested, a little too helpfully.

"I think it could be," Jacob said. "She doesn't know, so I don't know."

Stacey and I looked at each other.

"So either a group of people slipped in here, unnoticed, grabbed Catherine and her sons and drowned them all at once, or a powerful entity did it," I said.

"Isaiah," Stacey asked. "It fits. She kills him, then he kills her a couple weeks later..."

"And he kills the three kids?" I looked at Jacob. "What about the little girl?"

"Little girl?" Jacob shook his head. "I haven't seen one."

"Maybe she managed to move on, and she's not trapped here like the others," I said. "I hope so, for her sake."

"What's this?" Jacob walked to the little cottage at the back of the yard, the one that looked like a one-story model of the main house.

"Tool shed," I said. "I don't think it's locked."

He opened the front door, flanked by thin little fake columns that mimicked the ones by the real front door to the big house. They supported a little mock balcony above the door, just big enough for a cat or small dog.

He stepped inside, not flipping on the light, and stood there quietly, as if absorbing otherworldly vibes from the leaf blower or the hedge clippers.

"Anything?" Stacey asked. I was curious, too. Maybe Eliza's ghost had wandered over to the small version of her former home. It was certainly much calmer and quieter than the real house.

"Something happened here," Jacob said. "I want to say a ritual or some event that opened a door."

I nodded a little, thinking of Juniper and her attempted séance with her boyfriend on Halloween. I didn't say anything, though.

"Yeah." Jacob walked to the back, where there was an open space in front of a tool bench. "Right around here. It really jolted the spirits awake. Especially the woman by the pond, but also everything inside the house." Jacob walked back to the mini-front-porch of the tool shed and pointed to the pond. "She's been trying to get inside ever since, trying to reach her children. She uses…this is weird, but she tries to use the water lines to get inside. Like she can't use doors or windows, those are blocked to her, so she tries to sneak in through the pipes. Still, it won't let her inside."

Maybe the mystery of the dripping faucets had been solved, I thought.

"What's blocking her?" I asked, since he hadn't yet made that clear.

"Something strong," Jacob whispered, fairly dramatically.

"Is it the big, scary evil guy from the second floor or not?" Stacey asked, looking impatient.

"Maybe."

"That's her husband," Stacey said. I shook my head—as with zoo animals, you're not supposed to feed the psychics. Not information, anyway. Jacob's psychic check-up of the house was just about done, though, and I sympathized with Stacey's frustration.

"Interesting," was all Jacob said. He took a deep breath and stretched. "That's about it, guys. Unless there are secret rooms somewhere you haven't mentioned."

"Not this time, I hope," I said. "There's always bad stuff in the secret rooms. Let's go inside. Maybe Crane can tell us something new before he goes to bed."

"Can you try to talk to him, Jacob?" Stacey asked. "I bet he'll talk to you."

"I don't know. I'm not like a child psychologist over here." He looked worried as he returned inside with us.

"You'll be great," Stacey said, with so much confidence that even I half-believed her.

Chapter Sixteen

The family had gathered in the living room after dinner, and they were arguing about what to watch on television when we walked inside. Something about a malevolent, dangerous ghost infesting a house can really bring the members of the household together, at least in a physical sense. It's safer for the family to camp out together by the living room fireplace than to sleep separately and face the darkness alone. You get a glimpse of what life may have been like for our hunter-gatherer ancestors, everybody huddled near the communal hearth, scared of unnamed things in the dark world beyond their little spot of light—trying to entertain each other with stories and music so they forget about the predatory dangers lurking in the night outside.

"What'd y'all figure out?" Toolie asked, glancing from me to Jacob.

"He saw the same entities we've encountered," I said. "The Ridley family, I think."

"Did you see Noah and Luke?" Crane asked him.

"Are those the two boys in the attic?" Jacob asked.

Crane nodded. "Did you see the bad one upstairs?"

"Yes. I think Ellie and Stacey are going to get rid of him," Jacob said.

"I hope so." Crane was being extremely talkative tonight. Everyone else fell quiet, listening to the psychic boys talk. It was as if the stage lights had gone down for a moment, leaving just the two of them in their own world.

"Have you ever seen the little girl?" Jacob asked him.

"That's their sister," Crane said. "Did you see her?"

"No, where is she?"

"She likes to hide. She hides *all* the time."

"Have you ever seen her?" Jacob asked. "Or heard her voice?"

"Nuh-uh." Crane shook his head, extra-emphatically. "They talk about her. She's a scaredy-cat."

"Do you have any idea where I could find her?" Jacob asked.

"No. Do you like dragons?"

"Sure."

"I have three dragons in my room." Crane slid off the couch and dropped to his feet. "Can I show him my dragons, Mom?"

I gave Toolie a big nod. Crane might open up more with fewer people around.

"Just pick up your Legos while you do it," Toolie said. "I'm tired of stepping on them."

"Come on." Crane grabbed Jacob by the sleeve and tugged him out of the room.

"What kind of dragons do you have?" Jacob asked.

"A green one and a red one. And a blue one."

"Have fun," Stacey said, with a great big smile. I wondered if she was watching him with the kid and thinking about how he might be as a father, possibly to the psychic children they might one day have together. Oh, Stacey.

"Well, he certainly seems to like your psychic friend," Toolie said, and her husband nodded.

"Jacob confirmed a lot of what we've found," I said. "I now think there's a good chance Catherine Ridley murdered her husband, probably to stop him from abusing their boys. And it may have been a spirit who drowned Catherine and her two boys, instead of a mom-and-kid murder-suicide situation. When Jacob spoke to Catherine's ghost, she said the attacker was invisible."

"Stars and stripes!" Toolie gasped, covering her mouth. "That's horrible. Is that ghost still here?"

"There are really two suspects," I said. "Isaiah Ridley's ghost, out for revenge. Or a poltergeist created by Eliza Ridley, the little girl. Any poltergeist Eliza created would have dissolved or gone dormant after her death, because it feeds on its creator's energy. So the original plan still seems best—get Isaiah out of the house and go from there."

"I like...the sound of...that," Gord said.

"Stacey and I will go up and light the trap," I said. "I have to recommend that the whole family sleep down here tonight, together, unless you can go and stay at a hotel or a relative's house." I couldn't risk Isaiah deciding to murder everybody out of anger at our intrusion.

"There's nobody nearby except my cousin over in Beaufort," Toolie said. "The hotels around here are too expensive. And...it's difficult." She glanced at Gord's oxygen tank. "We'll stay down here, and we'll pack a couple of suitcases so we can leave if things get too bad."

"Then Stacey and Jacob can stay down here with you," I told her.

"Where will you be?" Juniper asked me.

"Upstairs, ready to slam the trap."

"I can hang out with you if you want," she said.

"Thanks, but I'd rather you help keep an eye on your brother," I told her.

Juniper frowned and looked down at her hands.

"Sorry, it could get dangerous up there," I said. "So I don't want to worry about anybody else running around.."

She shrugged a little.

"I'll let you know if you can help with something, though," I added.

"Whatever. I don't care that much." She returned to reading the werewolf romance paperback in her hands. I could tell I'd hurt her feelings, but I didn't know what else to do. I wasn't going to put her in danger.

Stacey set up her laptop so she could monitor the cameras inside the crafts room, and she handed me a tablet so I could watch the trap, too. Then she headed upstairs with me.

"I had no idea dragons could fly spaceships," I heard Jacob saying from the open door to Crane's room.

"Dragons aren't real," Crane said. "Spaceships aren't real, either."

"There are real space shuttles and rockets," Jacob said.

"Yeah, but not *good* ones like in the movies."

Stacey grinned at the sound of Jacob's voice, but her smile faded when we approached the crafts room door. A soft, icy draft leaked out on all sides of it.

We clicked on our flashlights, and I pushed it open.

I stepped into the dark room and tried to turn on the overhead light, but nothing happened. I panned my flashlight back and forth as I approached the trap. Stacey kept close behind me, walking backwards, shining her light in the opposite direction so nothing could creep up behind us.

I laid my four little pieces of ghost bait inside the open trap, at the very bottom of the cylinder. One tiny iron locomotive, one very tarnished 1851 silver dime, two cufflinks.

Then I drew a long-nosed fireplace lighter from a strap on my utility belt, and I lit the three candles spaced in a descending spiral around the interior of the trap. The fire would attract the ghost, since they're usually hungry for energy, and the bait would pull its attention into the depths of the trap and hold it there for at least a moment.

It was all pretty standard ghost-removal procedure.

As I lit the third candle, I heard deep, ragged breathing from the shadows just ahead of me.

The dark shape shuffled toward me, more than a foot taller than me and smelling of earthy decay.

I swung my lit fire-starter at him, since I was already in the middle of using it. The flame cast a scattered red glow into the rough caverns of his broken face.

He took a ragged, throat-blown-open gasp and sucked all the fire from the lighter, turning it cold and dark.

I raised my flashlight with my other hand, slamming the bright white beam into his dark, sunken eye. His iris was a clear, lifeless color, and the pupil didn't even react to the sudden blast of light. It should have shrunk to a pinpoint.

He snarled with half his mouth, since the other half was mostly missing. He didn't like the light, but I didn't get the feeling it was going to chase him away this time.

With my elbow, I nudged Stacey in the back.

"What's up?" She turned around and sucked in a frightened breath, but she held her light steady while she added it to mine, torching the ghost as best we could.

"Back," I whispered. "Out."

Stacey clung close to me, holding her flashlight over my shoulder to keep it trained on the hideous apparition. We eased our way backward toward the door.

The ghost of Isaiah flickered out of sight.

Then it reappeared right in front of me, only inches away.

Stacey and I both took in a breath, but we kept moving.

Isaiah watched us, keeping himself completely, unnaturally still in a way that only dead things can. Then he opened his right hand and unrolled his long, leathery belt, encrusted with sharp buckles and prongs.

He advanced on us as we stepped out the door. Stacey and I backed down the hall, shoulder to shoulder, our lights held out in front of us.

The ghost crept all the way to the threshold of the open door, his belt lolling in his hand like a dog's tongue on a hot summer day.

We tensed, waiting for him to attack. My hand was on my iPod, ready to soak him in some Viennese choir music.

He stopped, and I could hear his ragged breathing. His presence in the doorway turned the entire hallway cold and gave the air a clammy feeling.

He watched us for a moment more, and then the door slammed. He'd stayed inside his lair, as far as we could see.

I ran to check the two cameras pointed at the door. If he'd stepped invisibly into the hallway with us, we weren't seeing any thermal evidence of it.

I finally had time to notice how hard my pulse was racing, and I made myself breathe deep to calm down.

"He's still in there." Stacey picked up the tablet she'd given me, with a splitscreen showing the thermal and night vision cameras pointed at the trap in Isaiah's room. She pointed to a vague profile that slid in and out of visibility. "He's pacing. I guess that's what he does when he's not out hunting the boys."

The moving purple-black mass was more obvious on the thermal camera, where it seemed to roll back and forth, very slowly, on a field of deep blue, since the whole room was cold.

"Go get Crane," I said. "Take him and Jacob back down with the family."

"Then I'll come back here with you," Stacey said.

"No, I want you with them until they go to bed," I said. "Then I want you out in the van."

"Ellie, it's too dangerous to be by yourself."

"It'll be even more dangerous if I get blindsided by the Attic Twins or the poltergeist, or anything else," I said. "I need your eyes all over the house."

"Okay. I'll use the cameras in the living room to keep watch over the family while they sleep."

"Good idea."

"Maybe Jacob should sit in the van with me, too," Stacey said.

I raised an eyebrow at her.

"And help me watch all the monitors," she added. "I mean, the clients just met him, they won't necessarily feel comfortable with him hanging around while they try to sleep."

"You've made your case," I said. "Is he planning to stay all night?"

"He told me he'd stay as long as we need him. He has to work tomorrow, but..."

"All right. Get moving. I need all my attention on the trap."

While Stacey went to collect Jacob and Crane, I arranged myself on my handy air mattress. I kept the tablet on my lap, and I held the trap's remote control in both hands. The remote's display screen told me the temperature and EMF readings inside the trap. So far, the temperature still matched the rest of the room, about forty-eight degrees Fahrenheit. Very chilly.

It had been risky to light the trap so late, but I'd hoped it would help draw Isaiah's attention to it. Sometimes ghosts take a very long time to notice things. They tend to be backwards-looking beings, focused on the drama and trauma of their own lives and deaths, seeing their own memories instead of reality.

It turned out I wasn't so lucky. While Stacey and Jacob kept the Ridley family company downstairs—it sounded like they were watching some kid's movie, probably trying to keep Crane calm—I sat at the crossroads of the upstairs halls and watched while the ghost faded in and out of sight on the night vision, pacing and pacing, passing back and forth before the burning candles inside the trap.

Chapter Seventeen

Stacey eventually told me over the headset that the family members were ready to sleep on their temporary campground down in the living room. She and Jacob went out to the van to keep watch on everyone and everything.

We were particularly concerned about Crane slipping off again in the middle of the night, but I doubted that the parents would really be able to sleep well under these conditions, anyway. They'd probably be up most of the night, worried and afraid.

I sat at the hallway intersection, watching my trap on camera. The remote control for the trap has one big red button you really can't miss. That's the only feature besides the little screen with the temperature and EMF readings from within the trap.

The trap can be automatically set to close once it detects signs of a ghost inside, but I'd set the parameters pretty high—a twenty-degree drop in temperature combined with an electromagnetic spike of six milligaus or more would make the trap slam shut. I intended to keep watch all night and close the trap myself. This ghost was much too dangerous for me to just set it and forget it.

The house grew quiet except for the rain pounding the roof and windows, plus occasional claps of thunder. The flashes of lightning grew brighter, the thunder louder and closer, but nothing distracted Isaiah from his pacing. I worried he wasn't going to notice the trap at all.

Stacey checked in...occasionally. Nothing much was stirring. The boys had barely appeared in the attic, much less strolled downstairs for some late-night activities. The poltergeist, wherever it was, remained silent and calm.

I drank Red Bull and waited.

I wondered what Stacey and Jacob were doing out in the van together. Sitting awkwardly? Chatting? Maybe the combination of boredom and attraction had led them straight into some actual kissing. I tried not to imagine them making out on the uncomfortable, narrow little drop-down bunk in the back of the van.

Maybe Stacey was right, and I would be better off dating somebody instead of spending my Saturdays with old novels and Uncle Ben's microwave rice. Who would I even date, though? And what kind of person? Most people look at me like I'm crazy when I tell them my job.

Still, a cat wasn't always the most fulfilling company. Maybe I could get another cat. Maybe, in just a few short years, I could become a full-blown crazy cat-collector lady.

Around one-thirty in the morning, I stood and stretched. Then I walked to the hallway bathroom for a quick break.

As I looked up from washing my hands, I saw a small girl standing in the mirror beside my reflection. She wore a dress with a pattern that looked like calico, but was all white. Her skin was pale white, too, and her colorless hair fell in curls around her face. She was elementary-school age, maybe eight or nine.

I immediately glanced to my side, but nobody was there. The girl only existed as a reflection.

"I know why you're here," she whispered, staring at me with white-on-white eyes.

"Eliza?" I asked.

"I want to show you something." She pointed toward the tub, where the blue shower curtain was drawn tight.

Feeling more than uneasy—my stomach was tying itself in knots, in fact—I walked sideways toward the closed curtain, keeping an eye on the little girl in the mirror.

I could hear water running, fast and hard, behind the curtain.

That sound hadn't been there before. The bathroom had been silent.

I grasped the edge of the shower curtain with a trembling hand, then hesitated, trying to mentally prepare myself for whatever horror lay on the other side.

"Go on," the image of Eliza whispered from the mirror. "Look."

I pulled the curtain aside. The shower rings on the curtain rod clicked together, one by one, above my head.

The water was running at full blast. The tub was already filled to the top, though it had only been running for a few seconds, as far as I'd heard.

It was so full that when I pulled the curtain aside, a flood of water sloshed out onto my boots and splashed across the bathroom floor like a wave crashing onto a beach.

I leaned down to turn off the faucet, knowing how much damage the overflowing water could do to my clients' antique home. As I did, the bathroom lights went out.

I stood and turned, trying not to lose my balance in the inch of water on the floor.

The image of Eliza remained in the mirror, now the only source of light in the room. She looked ghastly, as if her form were woven from a thousand glowing filaments, with her eyes, nostrils, and mouth left as blank black holes.

Those black-hole eyes were looking right at me.

She began to rise, as though levitating off the floor over there in mirror-world.

"This is how I killed all the others." Her voice echoed from the stone-tiled walls around me. Her words came out flat and monotone, the voice of a long-dead thing.

"Did you kill your family, Eliza?" I asked. That made no sense to me, unless the girl had extraordinary psychokinetic ability. Judging by how she'd been able to create a menacing poltergeist, though, maybe she really *had* possessed other abilities.

"Just like this." Her voice was an echoing whisper.

She vanished from the mirror, leaving me in darkness, and I quick-drew my tactical flashlight like an Old West gunslinger.

She hit me before I could click it on. Her energy slammed into me like a solid brick wall mounted on the grill of a runaway freight train.

My feet slid out from under me on the soaking-wet floor. I

toppled over backwards.

Right into the water.

The cold hit me hard as I landed on my back on the tub. My hand banged against the stone-tile wall. If the water had been just a notch colder, I would have been crashing into solid ice.

Her voice echoed again, but it didn't sound dead and flat this time—it was a gleeful shriek, ricocheting off the bathroom walls.

Something slammed into my chest, just below the base of my throat, and shoved me under the frigid water.

My face went under, and I barely managed to take a breath on the way down.

An invisible hand pressed down on the crown of my head, holding me there as I tried to flail my way up and out of the water. It was too strong. I was trapped, and the meager sip of air in my lungs was fading fast.

I lashed out with both hands, having dropped my flashlight somewhere along the way. I could feel a patch above where the air felt unnaturally cold and thick, but my fingers trailed right through it. There was nothing solid to grasp. This is why you don't want to get into a wrestling match with a ghost.

A painful pressure built in my chest and my head. I could feel my struggles weaken and my arms start to go limp.

My lips wanted to open and suck in air, but I'd die instantly, my lungs filled with near-freezing water. I had to resist.

Spots floated behind my eyelids. This was it, killed by an evil child-ghost in a bath tub. Aunt Clarice from Virginia would never understand.

For a moment, I thought I saw the chiseled, high-cheekbone face of Anton Clay, the ghost who'd killed my parents in a house fire. His irises were red, and a devilish smile played on his lips.

"Now," he whispered.

I felt a sudden electric jolt in my ears, followed by a searing pain in my right ear that spread to engulf that whole side of my head.

My headset. It must have shorted out underwater and fired a nasty shock from the right earphone, where the microphone and battery wire were located.

Now I'd learn what it was like to drown *and* get electrocuted at the same time.

All the pressure holding me in the tub evaporated. I pushed my head out of the water and took a deep gulp of sweet, cool, fresh air.

Maybe the electric shock had stunned the ghost, too, interfering with her electrical field somehow. If so, I wasn't going to count on it to last long.

Feeling my way around in total darkness, I found the faucet and hauled myself up until I was sitting on the edge of the tub. The girl was no longer providing a helpful unholy-white glow to help me see.

She shrieked again, her voice echoing.

I dropped to the flooded floor and rolled onto my stomach. I wasn't eager to regain my feet on the slippery tiles, which would just make it easy for her to shove me into the water all over again, especially in my current weakened state. I was still gasping desperately for air.

She grabbed at my limbs, but I hugged the floor. It's a classic act of civil disobedience—refuse to obey or cooperate, no matter what. If they want to move you, turn into dead weight, make them use as much of their energy as possible.

I began to advance through the water, flat on my belly like a Marine in boot camp.

She seized a big handful of my hair and twisted it, sending shooting pains all through my scalp. I cried out in pain, but she had bigger plans than just hurting me.

She slammed my head face-first into the water on the floor, which was just deep enough to cover my mouth and nostrils. They say a child can drown in less than an inch of water. I guess I can, too.

With a great effort, I managed to turn my head sideways. I could now breathe out of one corner of my mouth, but I couldn't open my lips wide enough to scream for help.

I kept wriggling forward, wondering which device on my belt might short out next. I was guessing the iPod speaker. It could hit me with a nice shock right to the torso.

At last, my fingers found the rough wooden surface of the door. All I'd done was crawl across the bathroom, but it felt like I'd just swum the English Channel.

With all my strength, I shoved myself up to a swaying position on my knees, then felt my way up to the doorknob.

The door opened all by itself, the edge of it cracking into my face at high speed. I heard a pop in my nose, then tasted blood on my lips.

I tumbled back against the bathroom vanity. She'd hit me pretty hard, but she'd also let the water out and allowed in a little bit of light from the hallway. The pool of water spread out across the hallway floorboards and lapped against the baseboard on the far side.

I grabbed the edge of the door, determined not to let it close again, and crawled out into the hall.

She screeched a third time. I felt a cool breeze as she flew over my head, but I didn't see her. She'd turned invisible.

The night vision camera that had been sitting on its tripod in the hallway, pointed at the faucet inside the bathroom, lifted from the ground and flew at me. I rolled to one side before the heavy camera smashed into the floor where I'd been.

Further down the hall, a kind of whirlwind swept up all my gear. The thermal and night vision cameras pointed at the crafts room door exploded as if they'd been blasted with a high-caliber shotgun at close range. Their tripods clattered to the floor.

Everything else—my mattress, my toolbox, my tablet, my purse, my spare flashlight—slid away down the least-used hallway, the one that housed the two guest bedrooms. They stopped just before they reached the narrow side staircase that led down to the first floor.

I tensed, waiting for her to swoop back and attack me. By habit, I reached for my flashlight, but of course it wasn't there. I wasn't sure I could count on the music-blast approach to work, either. The speaker on my belt seemed waterlogged and would probably fry if I tried to switch it on.

My flashlight was still in the bathroom somewhere, and I definitely wasn't going to do her the favor of putting myself next to the Overflowing Tub of Death again. If she wanted me to return to that room, she'd have to drag me kicking, screaming, and biting.

Footsteps echoed on the narrow steps at the end of the hall. More than one person, as if Eliza had invited her murderous big brothers to join her.

I tensed. Virtually unarmed, I figured my best move was probably going to be running like crazy.

"Ellie?" a voice asked. Female, and not ghostly.

Stacey and Jacob clambered up the stairs, Stacey looking a little scared. She relaxed the instant she saw me.

"Oh, sweet!" she said. "I lost your signal." She tapped her headset, then seemed to notice I was dripping wet. "What happened?"

"I decided to take a quick bath." I untangled my headset from my soaked hair. My right ear still had a tender, burning feeling from the shock, and it also had a ringing sound that made it a little difficult to hear what she was saying.

"You had a bath, seriously?" She frowned a little, confused. "You look pretty banged up."

"No, not seriously. That was just me being hilarious. I met Eliza's ghost and she tried to drown me."

"Holy cow!" Stacey gasped. She and Jacob walked carefully around my stuff scattered all along the hallway. "Are you okay?"

"I'm still breathing."

"Good." She embraced me. Stacey's more of a hugging type than I am.

"Looks like the ghost did some redecorating, too," Jacob said, stepping around my mattress.

"I think these two cameras might have malfunctioned or something, because I lost the signals..." Stacey pointed to the cameras monitoring Isaiah's door, and she noticed they were broken into a hundred pieces. "Oh, yeah, that'll do it," she said.

"She's a nasty one. Murdered the whole family." I finally returned to the bathroom and recovered my flashlight. The remote control for the trap, which I'd set down on the bathroom counter while I washed my hands, now lay facedown on the wet floor. I hoped it hadn't fried like my headset.

I picked up the remote and turned it over.

The display screen was blank.

"I guess this one's ruined," I told Stacey as I returned to the hallway. She and Jacob were headed straight for Isaiah's door. "Stop! What are you doing?"

"Oh, did you miss the whole show?" Stacey asked.

"What show? I was busy with my own show. It was about bathroom safety."

"We got him," Stacey said. "He took the bait."

"When?"

"Just a minute ago. The trap sealed up—I thought you'd done it."

"It had to be the automatic sensors," I said. "Isaiah was inside? You're sure?"

"I can show you the video," Stacey said. She opened the door, and we followed her inside.

Chapter Eighteen

The crafts room still felt cold and clammy to me, but Isaiah's presence had been strong, and it would leave residual energy for a while even if he was gone. It was a dark spiritual residue, like a layer of rank oil coating everything. The light switch still didn't work, so all three of us held flashlights.

"See?" Stacey pointed at the stamper, which had slammed down the lid and closed the trap.

"It's definitely been sprung," I said, leaning closer to inspect it. "I'd like to have a look with my thermal goggles."

"We saw it all on thermal," Stacey said. "That purple-black cloud shrank and condensed into the trap. He totally took the bait."

I looked at the little items on the bottom, the rusty miniature locomotive, the old silver dime.

A thin curl of darkness hovered in the air just above the locomotive, like a loose thread taken from a black thundercloud. As I gazed at it, it twisted and disappeared, in a way that reminded me of how Isaiah had turned away and vanished the first night I'd seen him. He'd made himself invisible.

He could hide, but he couldn't run.

I lifted the trap out of the stamper.

"We still have a few more ghosts to hack through," I said. "But job one is to get this monster out of our clients' house. Let's take him down to the van. Then I want to review that footage, Stacey."

"It's good stuff. We should put it on our website," Stacey said.

"We don't have a website."

"We should have one!" Stacey said. "And a Facebook page, and definitely Flickr. And a YouTube!"

"Let's talk about it later," I said. Much, much later, I thought.

We carried the trap down the hall, past the camera wreckage strewn all over the floor.

"Jacob, sensing anything?" I asked. "Hit me with some psychic news."

"I think you got the nasty thing out of that room," he said. "It's still pretty bad in there, but it'll clean up. I can't say anything else in the house has changed..."

"We're not done yet," I told him.

As we reached the main stairs to the front hall, the trap slipped out of my arms. I thought I'd dropped it at first, and felt my heart sink a little as it banged against one of the steps below. I was still damp from the bath tub, so I was the last person who should have been carrying that trap.

It's the kind of detail that only becomes obvious once it's much too late.

Then the trap bounced up high, above our heads, until it smashed into the ceiling. That wasn't natural. It smashed itself along the molding, then careened downward through the air, bashed a hole in the wall, and then banged itself several times against a lower stair over on the middle flight of the stairway. It rose into the air and shook back and forth.

"It's like a Mexican jumping bean," Jacob said, watching with a slightly amused smile.

"Um, Ellie?" Stacey asked. "Have you ever had a ghost break out of a trap before?"

"That...really shouldn't be possible," I said.

The trap slammed against the wall again, then spun over the railing and sailed high in the air all the way down the hall, finally smashing into the wall above the front door.

Toolie, Juniper, and Crane already stood at the living room door, drawn by all the noise. They looked at the three of us charging down the stairs.

"What in the Lands' End catalog--?" Toolie began.

"Everybody duck!" I shouted, while Stacey and Jacob followed me down the last flight.

The trap hurtled down from the ceiling, rushed toward us, and crashed into the hardwood floor right in front of Toolie, giving the floor the kind of deep dent you might expect from an angry, stamping elephant. Then it flung itself against an old high-backed chair hard enough to crack the armrest.

It spun toward us, and we ducked as it sailed past and smashed through the glass pane of the back door under the second flight of the wraparound stairs.

Stacey and I reached the shattered door fast enough to see the cylindrical trap slam into the brick patio.

The lid blew off, and it was as if someone had smashed open a tank of liquid nitrogen.

Cold white smoke flooded the patio in an expanding circle, turning the layer of rainwater coating the bricks into a thin sheet of ice. More ice encased the wet patio furniture, and rows of icicles formed on the slats of the wooden chairs and tables.

A powerful gust of freezing air rushed in through the broken door, blowing my hair straight back. It felt like a blast of wind from an arctic hurricane.

It carried with it countless little raindrops frozen into glittering beads of ice. These pelted Stacey, Jacob and me like buckshot, nicking our hands and faces while we tried to dodge aside.

When the wind stopped, we glanced around the hallway, waiting for the next attack.

Toolie and Juniper stared at us open-mouthed from the threshold of the living room. Gord approached them, rolling his oxygen tank, and leaned against the wall.

Crane wasn't looking at us at all, but up at the wraparound staircase behind us. He slowly raised one pointing finger.

I turned to see Isaiah's ghost flicker up the second flight of steps, visible only for half a second before it vanished again. It flickered again on the third flight, then it was gone, probably down the upstairs hall and back to its lair.

"He escaped your trap," Crane said. A flat, toneless declaration.

"It looks like..." I didn't really know what to say, so I opened the shattered door, stepped over the broken glass, and retrieved the trap and lid from the rapidly dissolving layer of ice that covered the brick floor of the patio.

The lid was distended and puckered. It had taken great force to do that, twisting the hard plastic and the copper mesh until the trap was uncorked. The dangerous ghost had escaped like a genie from its bottle.

I carried the ruined trap back inside.

Everybody was looking at me—the family, plus Stacey and Jacob—obviously expecting me to have some answers.

I didn't have any. The best I could do was try to play it off and hopefully keep everyone from panicking.

I took a deep breath and sighed, trying to look frustrated rather than afraid.

"Looks like we'll have to do this the hard way," I said.

"What's...the hard way?" Gord asked.

"There's really no time to explain," I said, which was better than stating the truth: *I have no idea what to do right now.* "Stacey, we need to grab some gear from the van. Jacob, can you hang out here and keep an eye on the family?"

"Did that ghost really get out of the trap?" Toolie asked me.

"It did," I said. "But we're going to take care of it."

I tried to look as confident as possible while Stacey and I grabbed our umbrellas and walked out the door.

"What are we actually going to do?" Stacey asked while we trudged through the heavy rain. Sheet lightning illuminated the yard around us. The pond had grown to swallow most of the grass and now lapped at the brick patio like the edge of a lake.

"I sort of have an idea," I replied. "I don't know if it will work."

We gathered back in the living room, by the light of our flashlights, since all the power in the house was still off.

"Stacey, let's see if the camera in the hallway caught anything," I said. It was the only camera that the trap might have passed on its path of destruction, but it was aimed at the faucet in the powder room, so I didn't have a lot of hope.

Stacey grabbed the thermal camera itself from the hall, and I watched the display screen as she reversed the recording. She stopped when something flickered across the screen, then played it in slow motion.

The trap tumbled past in midair, its interior purple-black, filled with the ghost of Isaiah Ridley.

A greenish blob accompanied it. Blue spots speckled the green blob, growing larger as it expended energy flinging the trap around the hall and trying to pry it open.

The blob and the trap tumbled out of sight.

"It was the poltergeist," I said. I felt a little relieved—we hadn't met a ghost who could break free of a trap, at least. If we had, it might mean the traps were getting obsolete.

"Why would the poltergeist want to break him out?" Stacey asked.

"It's hard for me to find its motivation," Jacob said. "Since it was never human..."

"Maybe it needs the ghost of Isaiah." I looked up at the ceiling over the front door. The crafts room, Isaiah's lair, was just beyond the ceiling. "This is starting to make some sense."

"It is?" Stacey asked.

"Stacey, you're going to hang onto the ghost cannon." We'd brought the enormous, powerful, generally unstable and unreliable device in from the van. It was a hefty but allegedly portable source of light, bigger than a bazooka, with as much lumen-power as a Vegas spotlight.

"Cool," she said. I helped her strap on the heavy battery pack, which she had to wear on a harness on her back. "We're going up to his room, then?"

"You're staying down here to protect our clients," I said. "I'm taking Jacob with me."

"But I want to come with you," Stacey protested.

"That's an *order*, Stacey."

"Affirmative, generalissimo." Stacey gave me a mock salute.

"I can come with you and help out," Juniper offered.

"I'll call you when I need you," I told her, just to pacify her. I had no intentions of bringing her upstairs until the house was safe. The girl could be mad at me later, but at least she'd be unharmed.

I took Stacey's speaker and iPod, since she had the ghost cannon to protect herself and the others. I made sure I had two tactical flashlights on my belt and Jacob had a third.

"Are you going to...go after him?" Gord asked me, while I strapped my thermal goggles onto my forehead.

"You can't beat him," Crane said. "He's too strong."

"Thanks for that big vote of confidence," I said. "Don't worry, I've faced tons of ghosts like this before." Not exactly tons. Maybe a handful as scary as Isaiah Ridley. That's why I still preferred to think of him as Whippy McHalf-Face. "Come on, Jacob."

"Good luck," Stacey said, looking between both of us. She looked like she wanted to hug us, but fortunately she didn't—it would probably give the clients the idea that we were in lots of danger and weren't entirely sure what to do. We wouldn't want them thinking that, especially if it was true.

Later, there would be time to tell the family about the girl I'd seen and how she'd tried to kill me, but for now I wanted to hurry up and act, wanted to just deal with the problem without explaining myself every step of the way.

I grabbed the final big piece of gear I needed—a new ghost trap, taken from the rack in the van. The one wrecked by the poltergeist could probably never be trusted again.

Jacob and I started up the wraparound staircase together, shining our lights into the waiting darkness above.

Chapter Nineteen

There's something about walking through a house, any house, at night by the glow of a flashlight. It makes you feel like an archaeologist discovering some forgotten place, maybe the home of people who fled to escape a disaster like Pompeii during the eruption of Vesuvius.

The upstairs hallway was silent. Our footsteps creaked and echoed on the old hardwood.

Ahead, I could see our smashed gear strewn all over the hallway, spread much wider than it had been before, as if the poltergeist had come through in another big whirlwind.

"So, Jacob," I said, in the quietest voice I could manage, "Do you have a girlfriend?"

"What?" he asked. He gave me a surprised, curious look.

"Does 'what' mean yes or no? Or are you asking me for a definition of the word?"

"Should we be talking about that right now? Aren't we on our way to face some dangerous killer ghost? What are you expecting me to do?"

"I'm always on my way to face some dangerous killer ghost," I said. "I'm allowed to have conversations about other things. So which is it?"

"Which...? Oh, no. No girlfriend." He paused at the crossroads of the two hallways, looking at my stuff scattered along it, my mattress and camping pillow blocking the head of the stairs now, as though someone had decided to make a fort there. My guess would be the two boys from the attic.

"Do you date girls?" I asked.

"In theory. Not really since the plane crash..." He was talking about an airline crash in which he'd been one of very few survivors, and had awoken to find himself seeing ghosts everywhere.

"Are you going to ask Stacey out?"

"I...maybe. Do you think she's interested?"

I scowled. "Aren't you psychic?"

"Not about everything. Or I'd be winning lotteries all day long."

We stopped talking as we approached the final door at the end of the hall. The air was noticeably colder and thicker, and I could almost see the darkness slithering out around the edges of the door. Isaiah was wide awake, an angry beast waiting for us in its own nest.

"You're going to search the room for another ghost," I whispered to Jacob. "I'll keep Whippy McHalf-Face distracted."

"Keep *who* distracted?"

"The ghost who just escaped. Isaiah Ridley. I'll keep him busy. You're going to look for the little girl ghost."

"So we're not trying to capture Whippy McFadden?" he asked.

"Mc*Half*-Face...it doesn't matter. There's nothing I can do about him right now. The best I can do is try to hold him off. You're looking for an eight-year-old girl named Eliza Ridley. I think you'll find her in one of the cabinets, but I'm not sure which one. She used to hide there when she was alive, and they found her body there, too."

"Good thing there's only about twenty cabinets in that room. What will I do if I find her?"

"Just let me know. Ready?"

He looked at the door. "There's nothing to be gained by waiting five or ten minutes, is there?"

"Nothing at all."

"That's what I figured." Jacob approached the door and grasped the handle.

"Wait," I said.

"I'm going first. Don't worry, the evil spirits will cower before our flashlight beams, am I right?" Jacob pushed it open and led the way inside.

A heavy, ice-cold shroud seemed to hang inside the room, darkening all the walls in spite of our flashlights. Even a flash of lightning outside brought barely a glimmer through the balcony doors and tall windows.

"Okay, go," I whispered.

Jacob opened a cabinet. It was crammed full of cardboard boxes and old shopping bags.

He sighed and began pulling the junk out, piece by piece, until he could touch the inner wall of the cabinet with his fingertips.

"Nothing here," he whispered.

A deep, ragged breathing sounded in the air behind me. I turned and pointed my light directly toward the shadowy corner where I'd heard it. I couldn't see anything, but Isaiah was definitely there, or somewhere in the room, watching me with a palpable feeling of loathing and hate.

I slid my thermal goggles down over my eyes.

While Jacob rummaged through another cabinet, I looked back and forth in the sea of dark blue air and saw the purple-black shape of Isaiah. He seemed to be pacing on the other side of the room, back and forth, back and forth, watching us like a wolf in a cage. Unfortunately, there was no actual cage to hold him away from us.

I heard footsteps approaching and turned my head toward them, but I kept my light on Isaiah's ghost.

The door creaked open.

"Ellie, are you in here?" a voice whispered, while a glowing red-and-yellow shape looked in at us.

"Juniper?" I asked. "What are you doing?"

The purple-black mass of Isaiah surged across the room, straight toward the warm-blooded shape of Juniper.

"Get behind me!" I shouted. I drew my second flashlight and pointed it at Isaiah, joining its beam to the first one.

Juniper obeyed, running over to stand between Jacob and me.

"What's happening?" I whispered, assuming something had gone horribly wrong downstairs.

"I told them I was going to the bathroom and I snuck up here," Juniper told me with a triumphant smile.

"Why?"

"I thought you were kind of telling me to do that."

"What?" I asked. "No, definitely not."

"Do you want me to go back?"

Not with Isaiah lingering near the door, watching you. "You'd better stay with us. Point this right where I show you." I passed her a flashlight.

Juniper took a sharp breath.

"What is it?" I whispered.

She didn't answer—she was tense and still beside me.

"Can you see him?" I asked.

"Uh-huh," she whispered back. She was looking at the narrow stone fireplace where the cold form of Isaiah stood.

I raised my thermal goggles onto my forehead. Isaiah was visible in our overlapping beams, coated in dark earth, his chest rising and falling with his ragged breaths. The whip dangled from his right hand, its strange array of buckles glinting.

"Keep your light on him," I whispered, but it was obvious the flashlights wouldn't be enough this time. He was telling us that by standing there, making himself fully visible to us. Isaiah's ghost wasn't much of a talker, but he was sending us a threatening message with this apparition.

Blasting him with some loud orchestral holy music might have chased Isaiah away, but Jacob was still searching for Eliza's ghost, and I didn't want to startle her or send her deep into hiding.

"I found her," Jacob whispered. "This is the one."

"Okay. Juniper, come on." I took Juniper's arm, and she jumped a little bit, but then let me guide her backwards to the wall. "Keep your light on him. Can you do that?"

Juniper nodded, her mouth open, not daring to make a sound or even to look away from the dark ghost.

I glanced at Jacob, who knelt by a deep, empty cabinet, having dumped out the boxes and garment bags that had filled it. His palm rested on the cabinet's worn wooden floor, his fingers splayed.

"This one," Jacob whispered. "Definitely."

"Can she hear me?" I asked.

"She might, but you won't hear her. She's very faint, barely there. She's fragile, no strength at all, the most fragile ghost I've ever—"

"Get up and hold my light," I whispered.

As I passed him the flashlight, our fingers brushed together. Something jolted me, as if he were filled with static electricity.

Then—

I lay in my hiding spot, my knees tucked up against me. I hold my doll.

Through the door, I hear Mother and Father shouting. It's strange. Mother yells at us, but never at Father. Usually Father does all the yelling.

"Put it down!" Father was shouting. "A pistol doesn't belong in a woman's hand."

"We've had enough," Mother said. She was not yelling anymore. Her voice was calm and flat, but somehow that sounded much scarier. "Noah, Luke, and me. We've all had enough."

Then the explosion.

Then the silence.

Finally, I ease the door open. Mother has left the room.

Father lies on his desk. His face is half gone, and his papers are drenched in blood. His eyes are open and staring at me, lifeless.

I scream.

Later...many days later...I see them gathering firewood by the pond. Mother. Noah. Luke. None have wept for Father. None care that he is gone.

But I care. The pain rips at my insides, day and night. He is gone, and she killed him, and nothing is being done about it.

Then I feel it rise, the faceless thing that's tormented me. I feel it sweep out towards my mother and my brothers, as if carried along on the river of hate, fear, and sorrow that flows out from me.

Standing in the yard, I watch them drown, flailing in the water. My heart fills with fear. What is happening?

I run inside, upstairs to my hiding place, and close the door.

He's waiting for me. Father. He's seen what happened. His rage seethes in the air around me.

He's come to punish me, as he punished Mother and Noah and Luke, with his belt.

I feel it on my throat, leathery and cold, like a snake's skin—

"Ellie!" Jacob shook my shoulders, staring into my eyes. "Ellie, wake up!"

"Huh?" I blinked as if waking from a dream. "You did something to me."

"I'm sorry," he said. "I don't know what happened."

I turned to see Isaiah shuffling toward me, his steps jerky and unnatural. I'd glimpsed Eliza's memories, of course. That belt had just been at my throat, ready to strangle me.

I finally understood. Isaiah's ghost had murdered Eliza.

"Keep your light on him!" I told Jacob. "Now!"

Jacob took my place, standing shoulder-to-shoulder with Juniper and soaking Isaiah's ghost with white light.

I grabbed the new ghost trap and crouched down by the open cabinet.

"Eliza?" I whispered. "Eliza, can you hear me? I'm here to help. You can choose to escape this place forever."

"He's coming closer," Jacob said.

I slid the thermals down over my eyes again. At the very back of the deep cabinet, a few feet away, I could just discern a very faint, very pale blue shape, almost indistinguishable from the background cold of the room.

"Eliza," I said. "I understand you. I know what happened to you. All you have to do is step inside this jar. I'll light the way." I pointed the fireplace lighter into the trap and lit the three candles. "Just follow the candles to the bottom and rest there. I can take you to a safe place, full of trees and sunlight. You won't have to hide anymore."

Juniper let out a long, strange sigh, then collapsed to the floor. The flashlight rolled out of her hand.

"You okay?" Jacob turned his flashlight on the girl.

"Keep it on Isaiah!" I told him.

Jacob swung the light back toward the fireplace, but the dark figure was gone.

"I can't--" he began, and then a long, dirty leather belt, studded with buckles, cracked across his arm. It coiled around his forearm, lashing him hard enough to draw blood.

Then Isaiah snapped the belt, sending Jacob crashing into the sewing machine table, which toppled over in a heap of bright yarn and loose needles. Jacob went down in a heap of sewing and knitting supplies.

I was failing everyone tonight.

I checked Juniper, lying quietly beside me. She was unconscious, and her pulse felt weak.

The cabinet door slammed beside me. The girl I'd seen in the mirror earlier stood in front of it, arms crossed, giving me a petulant look. She was still white-on-white skin, hair, and calico dress, glowing with a soft, eerie light.

"What are you doing in there?" she said, in a whiny sort of tone. "Stay out of there."

"Leave us alone," I replied.

"You don't tell me what to do. This is my house."

"You're not Eliza," I said. "You wear her face because you were made from her anger and grief, but you're a thing that shouldn't exist. You're a poltergeist."

"What did you call me?" she whispered.

"A poltergeist. Normally, Eliza would have grown up, and you would have dissolved. But she never grew up, and her ghost was trapped in this house, so you still exist. But you shouldn't."

The girl scowled. When she spoke again, her voice echoed from all the walls. Chairs and boxes overturned, cabinet doors opened and slammed, and the window curtains flapped and snapped like sails in a storm.

"You do not know what I am," she said.

Something like a large, invisible hook stabbed into me, just under the ribcage, and hauled me upward. I howled in pain, and then I was flung hard against the ceiling.

Being pinned against the ceiling by an angry spirit is a situation from which there is no easy escape. If I somehow managed to get free, I'd still fall about twelve feet to the floorboards. Unpleasant.

Isaiah himself was busy tormenting Jacob. Jacob was backed up against the wall, taking a bad lash across the chest. Then he stepped forward and shouted something at Isaiah, which made the ghost stagger back a step or two and disappear. Isaiah appeared several seconds later on Jacob's other side.

I couldn't see much more of their fight, because the poltergeist rose close to me until her face filled my vision. She looked almost angelic...and then her lips twisted down into a hideous scowl, the corners of her mouth reaching all the way to her chin.

"You do not understand me at all," she said, her voice hitting my ears with a force that made them ring, especially my already-injured right ear. "I am older than you. You think I am nothing, but I have had years to watch and listen. For so long, that was all I could do."

"You should leave this family alone," I said. "*Both* families, the living and the dead."

"They are mine!" she snapped. "Because of you, I must kill everyone in this house tonight. You'll die first." She bared her teeth, and strange, guttural giggling burbled up from within her.

She reached her small, glowing white fingers into my throat.

I felt pressure, and I couldn't breathe. I struggled, but my whole body was pinned into place, the back of my head flush against the pressed-tin ceiling.

"You are so arrogant," she hissed. "You thought of me as nothing but an animal."

There was a gurgling sound in my throat, then a painful pop. Was that my larynx crushing or my windpipe rupturing? Only my coroner would know for sure.

"I've been watching and listening to you, too," she whispered. "I will collect my new family, and I will collect your friends. But I won't kill *you* inside my house. You can haunt the front garden. I'll keep you outside like a stray dog, just like *her*." I assumed she meant Catherine Ridley, the lady of the back yard pond.

I couldn't ask, though, because my vocal apparatus wasn't exactly free to function. In fact, there was a distinct lack of oxygen in my brain, and things were going dark. I wanted to tell the poltergeist that if she didn't want me to die inside her house, she would need to alter the situation fairly quickly.

As if hearing my thoughts, she pitched me across the room. I crashed into the glass double doors and out onto the balcony. I hit the rough brick floor and kept sliding.

I didn't stop until I slammed into the iron railing at the front.

Actually, I didn't stop then, either. My body was pushed against the railing, then began to slide upwards. She was trying to drag me up and over the top so I could fall to the brick steps below.

I grabbed one slender post of the railing, but it was slick with rain, and my grip barely slowed my ascent. I grasped it tighter as I reached the top of the railing. I hung there, barely clinging in place, while the rain pounded down on me.

A flash of lightning illuminated the house. When it faded, the poltergeist floated before me, softly glowing, still in the innocent little-girl shape of Eliza. She was on the outside of the railing, and she was gripping my arm and leg with her little hands.

"Let me go," I croaked, fighting her as she tried to pull me up and over the edge. My legs slid up to the top, but I managed to hook one foot under the railing. My heart was pounding too fast, like it was going to break right out of my ribs.

"You should have left me alone." She leaned in close, an expression of evil glee on her face. "Now you'll be my prisoner. My most hated pet."

She gave a hard tug, and I flipped over the top of the wet railing.

I managed to cling to the outside. The drop below was at least fifteen feet, and I had a feeling she'd give me an extra push on the way down, just to make sure my head split open against the front steps.

She floated alongside me, obviously not worried about the long drop below.

"I will torment you for years," she said. "For centuries. That will be your punishment."

"That's all you can think of, because you're nothing but leftover anger and wrath," I said. "You have no soul. You are *not real*."

"How dare you." She hissed as she floated above me. She gave me a hard downward shove, with crushing force.

I tried to resist it, but all I had was a feeble grip on the slick railing.

She grabbed my little finger and peeled it back. Then my ring finger. She was prying my fingers loose, one by one.

Thunder crashed again. The poltergeist-girl looked perfectly dry, every white-blond hair in place, the rain falling right through her.

With another weird, throaty giggle, she pried my middle finger loose. Now I was only holding on with my thumb and forefinger. My foot was still hooked under the top of the railing, but she'd be able to pull that loose with a little more effort.

My other hand grasped the railing from the outside, and I didn't think it would hold my weight if I suffered another hard push from above.

I couldn't believe I would die like this, dragged off and killed by a poltergeist. They're typically the mindless puppies of the paranormal world, knocking things and breaking them with no real sense of direction or purpose—just disorganized, chaotic kinetic energy.

This one had lived far too long, become self-aware, and created some plans of its own.

"I will enjoy watching your skull shatter," she said, her face twisting in a mask of anger and hate. "I will enjoy...enjoy..." She made a gagging sound and reached for her throat.

"Having problems?" I asked, feeling the first glimmer of hope.

"What...what..." Her head snapped back and forth, as if she were emphatically saying "no" and having a series of muscle spasms at the same time.

"I told you, you shouldn't exist," I said. "You only endured so long because Eliza's ghost was trapped in this house. That's why you've been protecting Isaiah. He keeps people out of that room, and he scares Eliza into staying right where she is. A hundred and sixty years in that closet, with you sucking out whatever strength she had. That's all over now."

The poltergeist twisted at the waist, her body elongated as she turned to look back at the open doors behind her.

"It's too late," I said. "Eliza is beyond your reach now." From the way the poltergeist was suffering, I could only assume Jacob had convinced Eliza to enter the trap, then sealed her inside.

The poltergeist turned back to me. Cracks spread all over her face, torso, and arms, as if she were a cheap plaster statue breaking apart in the rain.

"Now you've been uprooted," I said. "Your time is over."

The poltergeist screeched and lunged at me, moving so fast that her face and body blurred and distended. Her hands reached for me like little claws.

If she was going out, she was going to take me with her.

I tightened my grip on the railing, for what it was worth.

As she reached me, she exploded.

I don't know how else to describe it. The cracks in her face and body widened, then blew open altogether, shattering her.

She let out a high-pitched wail that could have made my ears bleed. My ears had been through way too much tonight.

A huge pulse of light erupted from her core, lighting up the stormy night like another bright flash of lightning. It swelled, pushing out force in all directions, nearly knocking me off the railing anyway. One end of the railing snapped loose, and the section where I clung tilted out and away from the balcony, leaving me dangling over the bricks below.

The glowing explosion swept over me and over the house, too. The unleashed poltergeist energy blew off window shutters, cracked panes on every floor, and dug deep furrows into the roof. Broken shingles sprayed into the sky.

The house shook as if a powerful earthquake were striking its foundations. This did not help with my slippery grasp on the loose, swinging railing, which bounced and shuddered while I hung on for my life.

The air felt stiff and hot, as though filled with static electricity.

Then the house ceased its quaking, the explosive light faded, and all was calm.

I started the pretty scary process of trying to climb back over a loose, slick iron railing in the middle of a pounding storm.

Chapter Twenty

I had just eased my toe over the top of the unstable railing when Jacob came running out through the balcony doors.

"Ellie?" he shouted, blinking against the heavy rain. He looked pretty tattered and bloody. Whippy had given him a very bad beating.

"Over here," I managed to say. He was already running toward me.

Jacob took my arms and lifted me over the railing. He set my feet on nice, solid ground.

I leaned against him, embracing him. Like I said, I'm not usually that much of a hugger, but he'd just saved my life, okay? It made me feel warm just to lean against him for a few seconds, letting him support me.

"You did it," I said, backing away from him a little. "Good work. Thanks."

"What did I do?" he asked.

"You convinced Eliza to go into the trap, and then you closed it. Right?"

"Me? I was busy getting my butt kicked all over the room by Whippy McFaddon."

"Whippy McHalf-Face," I said.

"Look what he did to me." Jacob held out one arm, the shirt sleeve ripped to pieces, the flesh lacerated and bleeding. "After that, I should be able to call him whatever nickname I want."

"Good point. But who caught the ghost, then?" I asked while we staggered inside, leaning on each other.

The room was destroyed, every piece of furniture overturned and smashed.

Juniper lay where I'd left her, on her side next to the cabinet door. Something was different, though—she now clutched the tall cylinder of the ghost trap in both arms.

"Juniper?" I shook her shoulder gently.

Her eyes parted just a little.

"Are you okay?" Jacob asked, kneeling beside her.

"I...I got her." Juniper gave an exhausted smile. "She's in there."

"Are you sure?" I gazed into the empty-looking ghost trap.

"Saw her do it. She came out like a mist, just a tiny mist..."

"And you closed the trap?"

"Like you were going to do," Juniper whispered. "Did it work?"

I glanced out at the balcony.

"It worked," I said. "You destroyed the poltergeist."

"What about the other one?" Juniper's eyes opened a little more, and I helped her sit up.

"I don't know." I looked at Jacob.

"Oh, Whippy?" Jacob asked. "After torturing me all over the room for a hundred million years, he vanished. It was right when that big explosion rocked the whole house. He isn't gone, I can tell that much. He's hiding somewhere."

"Ellie!" Stacey shouted from downstairs. There was panic in her voice. "Ellie, come down here!"

"Sounds like good news," I said, trying to ease the rising fear in Juniper's eyes. We helped her to her feet.

Out in the hall, I dashed ahead, leaving Jacob to help steady the exhausted girl. The poltergeist had drained Juniper like a battery.

I finally reached the far end of the hall, and I only had to descend a couple of steps before I saw what was frightening everybody downstairs.

Stacey stood near the foot of the stairs, shining her flashlight. Another beam, held by one of the family members I couldn't see from my angle, pointed in the general direction of both Stacey and the apparition.

It was a woman in a heavy woolen dress, thick with petticoats, and a matching kerchief. She was soaking wet, and as she ascended the first flight of steps, she left watery footprints behind her.

She walked slowly, like a recording moving at half speed, or somehow out of sync with our own reality. Each step took an agonizing amount of time.

I cautiously continued my descent, down the upper and middle flights. She'd barely climbed half of the bottom flight by the time I reached her.

"She came in through the door." Stacey pointed to the shattered back door below the stairs, from which rain spattered into the house. "I think she came from the pond."

The woman's face was cold and blank, like a porcelain death mask, but submerged below an inch or two of foul green pond water.

The pond water surrounded her like a nimbus, or like those hooded cauls in which some babies are born. It clung to her with no regard for gravity, other than the footprint puddles she left in her wake.

"It's Catherine Ridley," I said, standing two steps above the slow-moving ghost. "I'm pretty sure of it." She resembled the woman I'd seen faintly by the pond, but this was no faint, pale apparition. She appeared solid, three-dimensional, in full detail from her long blond hair—which floated in the thick layer of pond water on her shoulders—down to her leather winter boots.

Her eyes shifted to glance at me when I said her name, but she did not speak, did not react at all to my presence. She didn't seem to notice that the trap in my hands held her daughter's ghost, either. She just kept up her unnaturally slow steps, from one stair...to the next.

"Catherine, do you need some help?" I asked her.

She didn't reply. She was staring straight ahead as she walked right past me. I could see tangled, muddy weeds floating in the layer of water around her. The air dropped to near-freezing temperature as she passed, and I shivered, still dripping wet from the rain.

She turned...slowly...to begin the second flight.

Jacob stood at the railing by the top of the stairs, with Juniper beside him.

"Come on down, I think," I said. "Just hold tight to the railing. The stairs are getting pretty soaked."

I remained against the wall, easing sideways up the steps,

shadowing Catherine's ghost in case she suddenly attacked somebody. I doubted she would, but you could never be sure. I knew a thing or two about who Catherine had been in life, but I didn't know who she was *now*, as a century-and-a-half year old ghost, or what her intentions might be.

I had a pretty good idea, though.

When Jacob and Juniper had successfully slipped around the ghost without incident, we hurried downstairs to join the others.

"Juniper!" Toolie said. "Where have you been?"

"Up..." Juniper pointed, then let out a deep yawn.

"What happened out there?" Stacey asked. "That wasn't just lightning and thunder, was it? I thought the house was going to fall down on us."

"We detonated a poltergeist," I said. I touched Juniper's shoulder. "Actually, Juniper did."

"And I missed it?" Stacey frowned. "That would have been a great video for our YouTube channel. Jacob! What happened to you?"

"We don't *have* a YouTube channel," I said, but Stacey was already gushing and gasping over Jacob's many belt-buckle wounds, holding his arms to look at them more closely. She hadn't even asked about the sealed ghost trap in my hands.

Toolie and Gord were scolding Juniper for running off, but she seemed much too exhausted to care.

Catherine's ghost made her slow way up the second flight, still retaining a small pond's worth of water in the air around her.

"Where's Crane?" I asked, while placing the trap inside a coat closet. It would have to do for the moment.

"Oh, he's right..." Toolie pointed to the empty space beside her, then ran into the living room. "Crane? Crane? Where did you go? He's not here!"

"We need to search for him," I said, my brain shifting back into high-adrenaline mode. We hadn't done anything about the boy ghosts yet, and last I'd heard, they wanted Crane dead. They might have quietly lured him away to some other part of the house while we were busy dealing with the poltergeist. "Jacob, you go with Toolie. I'll take Stacey back upstairs. Juniper, stay in the living room with your dad."

"But I want to help..." Juniper gave another huge yawn and stretched. "Couch sounds good."

Toolie and Jacob went into the living room with Juniper and Gord. They would probably start there and move on to the library.

Stacey and I sloshed our way up the stairs, mumbling "Excuse me" as we passed Catherine's ghost, who did not acknowledge us at all.

I ran directly to the attic door and flung it open, shining my flashlight up along the steep stairs. Nothing immediately leaped out to kill me.

"Shouldn't we check Crane's room first?" Stacey asked.

"No." I hurried up the stairs, not caring how loud my footsteps echoed. Whatever the ghosts were doing with Crane, I definitely wanted to distract them from it.

Stacey and I shouted Crane's name, sweeping our flashlights through the darkness.

We didn't have to search long. He sat under the big plastic Christmas tree, next to the endlessly cheery life-size plastic Santa Claus. A wooden train full of toys, operated by a reindeer engineer, lay toppled over where Crane had made room for himself.

Stacey gasped and squeezed my hand at the sight of him.

He barely reacted when he saw us.

In his right hand, he held a broken Christmas ornament. It had once been a cut-glass angel, but one wing had been snapped off, leaving a long, sharp edge.

Red blood shimmered along the broken wing, and a drop of it had coursed all the way down the cut-glass robes into the angel's sandal.

Crane's left wrist was coated in blood, leaking from three deep scratches he'd apparently carved himself.

"Crane," I whispered. "What are you doing?"

"You can't help them," Crane said. "I have to help them. I have to join them."

"No, no, no," Stacey shook her head. "You totally don't have to do that."

"It's the only way to beat him," he said. "All of us together."

"You mean Isaiah? Their father?" I asked.

Crane hesitated, then nodded.

I eased forward. I wanted to grab the broken angel from his hand, but the way he was holding it, I could have sliced his fingers in the process. The entire situation was so wrong, trying to talk a seven-year-old kid out of suicide. Again.

"This won't work," I said. "Believe me, I know as much as anybody can know about ghosts, and this will not--"

"*Shh!*" a voice hissed, loud and angry, right in my ear.

Stacey cried out as something slammed into her, flinging her backward until her head cracked against one of those low-lying beams.

At the same time, something slammed into my ribs, knocking me into a pile of plastic jack-o'-lanterns, ghosts, and witches. I managed to climb up to my hands and knees, but then I was slammed into the stacks of cardboard boxes lining one wall. I couldn't move. The air was turning very cold.

"*Shh,*" the voice said again, near my ear.

"Quit shushing me," I said.

"*Quit,*" it whispered back, echoing me.

By the Christmas tree, Crane was digging the broken ornament into his arm again, carving a fourth red line.

"Crane, stop!" I shouted. "Stacey, can you hear me?" She was lying on the floor several feet away from me.

"Ugh," she said. "I can't move. Like somebody's sitting on me. Somebody with a really *cold* rear end."

"That's Luke," I said. "Or Noah."

Boyish laughter echoed in the air. It sounded menacing enough to me.

"Crane, put down that angel and run downstairs!" I shouted. "Go back to your parents!"

Crane looked at me with a glimmer of hope, as if this was just what he'd hoped someone would tell him to do.

"Go!" I repeated.

Crane stood, moving much slower than I would have liked. He held onto the ornament, but he took a step or two toward the stairs. I figured Noah and Luke couldn't restrain him without releasing either Stacey or me—there were only so many ghosts to go around.

"*Don't leave,*" a voice whispered, very close to me.

"*Help us,*" whispered another, over by Stacey.

Crane hesitated.

"Don't listen to them," I said. "You don't have to do what they say." I suddenly wished I'd brought Jacob instead of Stacey—the kid at least seemed to listen to Jacob. Jacob had been pretty banged up, though, so I'd given him the lighter duty of searching downstairs.

I hoped they'd decided to continue to the second floor.

"Jacob!" I shouted toward the stairs. "Toolie! Can anybody hear me? Come up to the attic--"

I gagged on something invisible. It felt like a rough, dirty cloth had just been shoved down my mouth and into my throat. I managed to cough and hack, but I couldn't speak.

Downstairs, the doorway to the hall slammed shut—I could hear it, but I couldn't see it.

Heavy footsteps clomped up the stairs. Stacey and I looked at each other, and I hoped I didn't look as afraid as she did. The footsteps didn't sound like Jacob or Toolie to me, and I don't think either of them would have slammed the door shut, anyway.

Stacey remained silent. She saw the figure on the steps before I did, and her eyes grew wide.

Isaiah's ghost became visible in profile first, a shadowy figure rising up behind the broken railing, his head shattered and smeared with earth.

"He's coming," whispered the voice near Stacey.

"Do it now," urged the voice near me. *"If he kills you, you'll be his. Not ours."*

"Do it."

"Do it."

Crane moved the ornament toward his wrist again.

"Don't do it!" Stacey yelled, only to have her face lifted and slammed into the floorboards.

Crane dug the sharp glass deep into his arm, with a look of determination on his face. Fresh red blood leaked out all over his arm.

I struggled, trying to yell for him to stop, and trying to get free. The boy-ghost wasn't nearly as strong as the poltergeist, but I'd *already* wrestled the poltergeist earlier that night, on two different occasions, and I was so dizzy and weak that I could barely cling to consciousness.

Isaiah stepped around the broken railing and walked directly toward Crane. Crane shivered, sitting down in front of the Christmas tree again, still cutting himself with the broken glass angel.

"Do it now," one of the boy's voices urged.

Crane winced as he stabbed himself deeper, ignoring Stacey's pleas for him to stop.

Isaiah towered over Crane. He opened his large, filthy right hand, and the long belt unrolled from it.

It looked like all the ghosts wanted Crane. The different ghosts may have wanted him for different reasons, but the underlying motive was probably the same: Crane seemed to have powerful psychic abilities, and the presence of someone like that can amplify a ghost's powers.

Maybe the two boys planned to use Crane to stage a revolt against their father, while the father wanted to use Crane to make himself stronger. It was only a question of whether Crane would kill himself and join the boys, or Isaiah would kill Crane and lay claim to his spirit.

Either outcome was awful and completely intolerable to me.

I kicked and struggled some more, and did my best to cry out, trying to distract Isaiah's ghost.

"*Shh,*" a voice said beside my ear.

"Hey, Whippy! I mean, Isaiah!" Stacey shouted. "Isaiah Ridley! Look over here, it's your boys. Don't you want to punish them? They're being really, really bad—"

"*Shh,*" both voices whispered.

The ghost's hold on me had relaxed enough that I could speak.

"Over here," I said, my voice a little croaky. "Isaiah, look, your boys are over here--"

I got slapped across the face for that. I slapped back, even though the boy holding me was insubstantial. Sometimes you just have to slap on principle.

Isaiah turned from Crane to look in our direction, his attention shifting to Noah and Luke.

Then he flickered a few times, but he didn't move anywhere. He kept appearing and disappearing right at the same spot.

Down the stairs, the door to the hall creaked open again.

"Jacob?" Stacey called.

Footsteps sounded again, but these were lighter and slower than Isaiah's could have been. They also had a wet, sloshing sound to them.

Catherine's ghost became visible through the broken railing, the pond water still surrounding her, as though she had to perpetually drown again and again.

She climbed up the stairs and turned toward her husband's ghost.

Isaiah flickered again, this time reappearing a few feet away, deeper into the attic. He flickered back and back again, retreating as

Catherine's ghost approached him.

She raised one hand high above her head, and Isaiah fell to his knees. He raised a hand, too, but in more of a defensive gesture, as if he expected a blow to his head.

His chest rose and fell, and he let out a weird, ragged sob.

"It's time," Catherine's ghost whispered. It was the only thing she'd said since walking into the house. "It's long past time."

Isaiah gave another sob when she reached for him.

The layer of pond water suspended around her hand hardened in the freezing air near Isaiah. Sharp icicles encased her fingers. She reached closer, and a paper-thin layer of ice formed along her arm, almost to her shoulder, with a cold crackling sound.

There was no poltergeist to protect Isaiah now.

Catherine's face remained dead-vacant, with no expression at all.

She stabbed the long, sharp icicle of her index finger directly into the hole in the left side of Isaiah's head, the exact place where she'd shot him a hundred and sixty years earlier.

Isaiah let out an agonized wail and rose to his feet.

Catherine turned and dragged her husband toward us, while he staggered and stumbled along behind her.

Stacey and I didn't dare move or speak as they passed us. Catherine still walked at her creeping-slow pace, but a couple of times, they ghostly pair flickered forward several feet at once.

When they reached the stairs, Catherine paused, forcing Isaiah to pause with her. She turned her cold death-mask face to look at us, and then she said the last words I would hear her say:

"Come, boys. It's time to go home."

Then she turned and started down the stairs, towing Isaiah's ghost along with her.

I felt the weight lift off me, and Stacey gave a cough and rolled up to a sitting position.

After Catherine and Isaiah began their descent, I finally had a glimpse of Noah and Luke. They were shadowy, filmy figures, walking with their heads hung low, trailing like obedient ducklings behind their mother.

Stacey and I both ran to Crane, who had watched all of this in wide-eyed silence, just like we had. Even then, I didn't want to speak for fear of distracting the procession of ghosts from their descent.

"Crane? Are you okay?" I whispered as quietly as I could.

Stacey embraced him, holding his head against her chest as if he were her own child. It had been hard to watch the little boy cutting himself.

I inspected his arm. Most of the scratches seemed shallow, practice cuts while he worked up his nerve. I was pretty sure there would be a lot more blood if he'd actually hit a major vein or artery, but I'm no doctor, and he needed to see one as soon as possible.

We tiptoed to the broken remnants of the railing and looked down. The four ghosts were on the landing, walking slowly at Catherine's pace. An eyeblink later, they were down the stairs, filing out through the door to the hall.

We followed them down.

Chapter Twenty-One

After we stepped off the attic stairs, we saw the procession of ghosts far down the second-floor hall, approaching the big central staircase.

Jacob and Toolie stood in the side hall where the children's rooms were located. They were staring after the apparitions, Toolie clinging to Jacob's arm.

"We're back," I whispered, startling both of them.

A horrified look crossed Toolie's face at the sight of Crane—wet with blood from his wrist to elbow, more drops of blood spattered on his shirt and jeans.

"Crane!" she ran toward him, taking his arm in her hands. "What happened?"

"I'm okay," Crane said. "It's over now."

Toolie ushered him off the to the master bedroom to wash and bandage his wounds.

Stacey, Jacob, and I continued after the ghosts, moving as slowly and quietly as we could manage, as they walked silently down the main stairway to the front hall. The entire situation had the eerie feeling of a late-night funeral march, but without a note of music or a word of prayer.

Downstairs, Juniper and Gord stood in the living room doorway, watching the ghosts walk by. Gord clutched his daughter's hand in one of his own. With his other, he squeezed the handle of his rolling oxygen tank in a white-knuckled grip.

They both gave me frightened looks as I descended the last stairs —where were their missing family members, and how were they supposed to react to a group of specters haunting their hallway?

I placed my finger to my lips. Above all, at that moment, I didn't want to interfere with the process of exorcism that seemed to be underway.

The shattered back door swung open again, sloshing through the puddle of accumulated rain on the floor.

The four ghosts blinked away, and then they were outside, shuffling toward the swollen pond that took up most of the yard. The four of us who were still living followed them at a cautious distance.

The ghosts grew blurry in the heavy rain.

Catherine, devoted mother and lethal wife, dragged Isaiah into the water, still moving in her slow but relentless way. A scrim of ice formed on the surface of the pond when Catherine pulled him under the surface. The thin ice melted quickly as fresh rain poured down on top of it.

Noah and Luke followed them down, one after the other, until the entire family was completely submerged in the dark water.

And then they were gone.

* * *

I sent Stacey and Jacob to turn on the power while the rest of us gathered in the kitchen. Toolie served iced tea. Crane's arm was fully bandaged, and he nibbled slowly on an Oreo cookie. Gord and Toolie sat with their kids while I leaned against the counter, feeling both jittery and exhausted. It was almost three in the morning.

"So the...poltergeist...was holding all the...other ghosts here?" Gord asked, while the lights flickered on overhead.

"Essentially," I said. "The poltergeist knew it was rooted here by Eliza's ghost, and if the ghost left the house, the poltergeist would have been destroyed. That's why it was protecting Isaiah's ghost, too. So once the poltergeist was gone, there was nothing to stop

Catherine from entering the house and finishing the job she began when she was alive—getting rid of her husband."

"That's so wild," Juniper said. She sat in a kitchen chair, her knees drawn up to her chin. "So if I didn't make the poltergeist, why was it bugging me?"

"It needed a new host," I said. "It needed someone living to feed on. This is a really strange case, because I've never heard of a poltergeist so old. It must have been dormant for a long time...and Catherine's ghost must have been dormant during that time, too. Something may have happened recently, maybe in October, that really jolted these spirits awake."

Juniper frowned. Her Halloween seance had likely awoken both the poltergeist and Catherine, which was another reason the poltergeist might have attached itself to her.

"It's my fault, too," Crane said. "I think I woke them up. I woke up the boys."

"You didn't intend to do it," I said. "Anyway, the ghosts have left the building. We'll need to return in a few days to check over the house, but after an exit like that...I'd say you're probably in the clear."

"The house certainly feels safer already," Toolie said. "Not so heavy and dark."

Crane nodded.

"And what happens to Eliza?" Juniper asked.

"We'll take her to a remote cemetery where she can be at peace," I said. "We know a few of them, and I'll bring her to the nicest one. Lots of old magnolias and wildflowers. Lots of songbirds and rabbits. She'll be much happier than she ever was here."

Juniper nodded, but she still looked troubled about it.

"So her father killed her?" Juniper asked.

"Her father's ghost," I said.

"But why? He really liked his daughter, right?" Juniper asked.

"The poltergeist looked just like Eliza," I said. "Maybe Isaiah's ghost witnessed the poltergeist killing his sons and thought it was Eliza. In his confusion and grief, he attacked his daughter instead of the poltergeist she'd created."

"It's just all so sad," Toolie said.

"And then there was light, huh?" Stacey said, entering the room with Jacob. She was blushing and he was smiling kind of awkwardly. I wondered what they'd been up to back there, besides tinkering with the power switches.

"And then there was sleep," I said. "Mrs. Paulding, I have to sweep up some broken cameras in the upstairs hall. We'll come back for the rest of our gear in the morning, if that's all right." The thought of collecting the cameras, microphones, and the heavy stamper was far too much. "That will give us a chance to do a quick check of the house, too."

"Of course, of course," Toolie said. "And I'll clean up the mess, don't worry about it."

"There's broken glass--"

"I'll take care of it. Go on." She sighed. "It's sad to think of those people trapped in this house for so long. Especially the kids."

"It is," I agreed.

"You figure they went off to Heaven? Or Hell?" Toolie asked.

"Those are two possibilities," I said. "The important thing is that they've moved on to wherever they're supposed to be. That's all we really know."

Toolie nodded, thinking this over.

We collected the ghost trap from the hall and headed outside.

"Five more ghosts, totally annihilated!" Stacey said, once we were on the driveway and away from the clients. "We should start a scoreboard at the office."

"Does the poltergeist count as a whole ghost? Or just half?" Jacob asked.

"*That* one should count as two or three ghosts," I said. "Thanks again, Jacob."

"Yeah." Stacey gave him a hug that seemed to linger for many, many extra seconds.

"Look, I'm happy to help you guys out," Jacob said, "But it seems like you always invite me in right at the evil-ghosts-ripping-people-apart stage."

"Maybe we'll invite you in earlier next time," I said.

"Yeah, at the boring library part," Stacey said. "You can squint through old deeds and tax records with us. You'd love it."

"I'm excited already."

I gave Jacob a quick hug, too. Saved my life. Nice guy. Cute, not that it mattered to me.

Stacey and I climbed into our van. While I waited for Jacob to pull out of the driveway, I couldn't help noticing that Stacey was humming softly and happily to herself in a way she usually didn't.

"What's with the singing?" I asked.

"Guess who finally asked me out." Stacey beamed at me.
Being a professional detective, I guessed it right on the first try.

Chapter Twenty-Two

"So that's your final story?" Calvin asked. We sat at the long table in the middle of our workshop, which includes soldering stations, a video-editing cubicle, and a big glass kiln, among other things that don't usually go together. There's also an espresso machine, which I'd bought Calvin as a fairly selfish gift one Christmas. He ended up using it more than I did, though.

It was Saturday, almost a week after we'd wrapped things up at the Paulding house. Stacey and I had returned to double-check the house the previous night.

"That's it," I said. "The father was abusive to the boys, the mother killed him. The little girl spawned a poltergeist that ended up killing her mother and brothers. She must have felt a lot of anger and resentment toward her family—she hadn't hated her father like they did. And the poltergeist ultimately acted out that anger in the most extreme way. Isaiah's ghost saw it happen, but thought the poltergeist was Eliza herself. That must be why he killed her—he blamed her for killing the boys. He probably had no idea what a poltergeist was."

"I told you, poltergeists made by girls and young children are the most dangerous," Calvin said. "I've found no cases of poltergeists being so long-lived. You might write an article about it for the

Journal." He wasn't talking about the Wall Street investment paper but the *International Journal of Psychical Studies*, the closest thing that exists to a trade magazine in our line of work.

"Why would I want to do that?" I asked.

"It could be good publicity for the agency."

"Stacey wants to start a Facebook page for us."

"I'm old enough to pretend I have no idea what that is," Calvin said. He gestured toward the two items on the table: a sealed ghost trap and a large rectangle wrapped in brown paper. "So you'll be releasing the girl?"

"I'm not sure she's in there," I said. I fetched him a pair of thermal goggles. "Look."

Calvin strapped them on and leaned close to the trap. "I see what you mean. Not a sign of activity. Jacob said the ghost was very faint, though."

"I think she might have moved on."

Calvin looked up at me, the goggles still strapped to his head. It made him look a bit like a cyborg, especially combined with the wheelchair. "Her choice to enter the trap was also a choice to leave the house, to let go of her life and death and move on."

"And move on." I nodded. "But the only way to check..."

"Is to open the trap." Calvin sighed. "All right. Set up a thermal camera, EMF meter, motion detector. And turn off the lights."

I hurried to arrange the gear. He watched through the thermal goggles while I set the trap to blow off its lid. Usually, I leave the trap in a carefully selected old cemetery and set it to open a couple hours after I leave—a little pocket of compressed gas opens the lid, freeing the ghost to wander its new residence. We do this for the ghosts that aren't a real threat to anyone, like Eliza.

This time, I set the trap to open in ten seconds, giving me just enough time to stand behind the thermal camera and watch.

The lid popped off with a hiss and landed on the table beside the trap.

I saw nothing on the camera, not even the slightest cold spot to indicate a ghost. There was no change in the EMF readings, either.

"No ghost?" I asked.

"No ghost." Calvin turned his head back and forth, scanning the room. "Not a thing."

"I guess she really did move on." I stopped recording and turned on the light over the table.

"One mystery solved." Calvin reached toward the package wrapped in brown paper. "Now will you tell me what's in the box?"

"There's some extra good news," I said. "A couple of days after we left, Gord found he was breathing much easier. He went to the doctor, and his emphysema seems to have vanished. They're still testing him, of course, but he says he has no problems now, no more feeling of drowning in his own lungs. He doesn't even use his oxygen tank anymore."

"That is good news. It sounds like his disease might have been a symptom of the haunting."

"It fit with the whole drowning and dripping thing going on in that house," I said. "Gord was so grateful, he created this for us."

"That's my cue to unwrap it?" Calvin asked.

"That's your cue."

Calvin tore off the brown paper wrapper.

Inside was a large painting, about three feet high, of an antique candy tin. The tin was labeled "GHOSTLY GUMBALLS" in big, cartoon-scary green letters. The image on the tin showed an apparently haunted gumball machine. Several pastel sheet ghosts floated around inside the glass globe. One mischievous little ghost was leaning out through the partially-raised candy door at the bottom, as though plotting his escape.

"That's fantastic," Calvin said, with an amused smile.

"I almost took it home without telling you about it. Where should we hang it? The front room?"

"I guess we could use a decoration of some kind out there. Good news about the client healing up, too."

"It makes me feel much better about sending an invoice. We kind of left their house a wreck, lots of damage."

"No more ghosts, though."

"No." I hesitated, then I told him about what had happened while I was drowning, the brief glimpse of Anton Clay with his fiery eyes. "Why do you think I saw him?"

"That's probably just your brain, flashing back to the first time your life was in danger," he said. "Inside the mind, time is based on feelings, not clocks. Whatever you feel most strongly about can seem very immediate, even if it happened many years ago."

"Just a memory," I said. I nodded. The alternative, the idea that Anton had somehow been able to reach out to me when I was on the verge of death, was too chilling to consider. It remained a possibility, though, with some chilling implications about how connected I was to that evil pyrokinetic ghost.

I stood up. "I'll hang the painting tomorrow. Stacey wants me to come to her apartment. She says it's some kind of emergency."

"She has an emergency and you've been sitting and chatting with me?" Calvin asked.

"I don't think it's a house-on-fire emergency," I said. "She has a date with Jacob tonight."

"Oh, good. Fraternizing among the staff. Nothing bad could come of it."

"Jacob's just a volunteer, though. So I guess he can date whoever he wants, right?"

"Whoever he wants?" Calvin raised his eyebrows. "Why would you phrase it that way?"

"What are you asking me?" I asked.

Calvin regarded me for a moment, then said, "What about your romantic life? Anything interesting on the horizon?"

"Nope. The horizon's all just empty sky."

"Maybe--"

"Please don't try to scrape up somebody for me to date," I said. Then I smiled. "I appreciate your concern, Calvin."

"I just don't want you to be lonely."

"Now you sound like my aunt. It's not your style." I kissed him on the temple as I left.

"Ellie," he said. "Don't let death consume your entire life."

"Thanks, Obi-Wan." I waved as I left the office.

Chapter Twenty-Three

"What do you think of this outfit?" Stacey asked me, turning in front of her closet. Stacey's room was decorated with her nature photography, like deer and hawks, and pictures of her family. Her kayak was stored near the ceiling, suspended on ropes. "Light summer dress over jeans?" she asked.

"Where's he taking you?"

"Blues in the park, supper at Moon River," she said.

"Lucky," I said. Moon River Brewing Company had some great kinda-organic American fare with lowcountry and Creole influences. "Watch for ghosts. That place used to be the City Hotel—it's *really* haunted."

"That'll give us something to talk about. So, should I wear this, or--"

"Wear that," I said.

"Seriously? Because I was also thinking--" Stacey reached for a shirt hanging in her closet.

"No, you nailed it the first time. Slam dunk. Hole in one. Other sports analogies."

"You really think so?" she asked.

"How would I know? Why don't you ask your roommates?" I

pointed toward the door. Beyond it, a couple of girls were talking and laughing in the living room. "I'm literally the last person to ask about fashion."

"Yeah, but you and Jacob are so alike," she said, dropping onto her bed beside me.

"We are?" It would be an understatement to say I was surprised by that idea. "Why would you think that?"

"Well, you know, y'all kind of have the analytical-left-brain thing happening."

"He's a psychic."

"And you're a ghost trapper," Stacey said.

"I prefer to keep it scientific, though."

"And he's an accountant by day. You see what I mean?"

I didn't. "So you're saying I should date Jacob?"

Stacey laughed. "No, I just want your opinion on what to wear."

"And now you have it. You'll have fun. It doesn't matter what you wear, you're pretty."

"Aw, thanks."

"Shouldn't I get out of here before he shows up?" I stood and moved toward her door. "It could get awkward."

"Why?"

"Just because, work talk, you know? Could be a distraction." I was feeling strange about the situation, getting into everybody's personal lives. "So unless you wanted to ask me about your shoes or something..."

Why did I say that? Of course she did, and of course she owned a heap of them.

Eventually, I got out of there, leaving through the gated front door as I stepped onto Abercorn Street. The sidewalk took me past old brick and stone houses with impressive columns and elaborately sculptured trim. These quickly gave way to smaller, less impressive houses, with wooden porch posts instead of neoclassical columns, some of them converted into little shops. Massive trees grew everywhere, screening the old buildings with yards of Spanish moss.

I felt weirdly jealous of Stacey. Not because of Jacob—maybe there had been that moment, right after he'd helped me off the balcony railing, when I'd felt something, but Stacey had always been interested in him. I wasn't so sure about dating a psychic. I can imagine several drawbacks...like possibly hearing my thoughts. No, thanks.

Still, I *was* jealous. I wished somebody interesting were taking me out that Friday night. Instead, I'd fold laundry with my cat.

It was dark out, and my senses were keyed up as I approached my car. The old black Camaro that Dad had bought less than a year before he'd died. His trophy car, celebrating some kind of promotion at his construction firm. I missed both my parents so much.

Walking along the streets at night in Savannah, it's not unusual to hear footsteps following you, only to turn and see nobody there. Or you might pass somebody in oddly old-fashioned clothes on the street, only to blink your eyes and have the person disappear entirely. Voices, music, laughter, screams—the past and present mingle freely here, as do the living and the dead.

As far as anyone could tell, I might have been just one more lonely ghost haunting the old city, paying no attention to those I passed, lost in my own memories.

I thought of my parents, and my friends, and Stacey offering to hook me up with one of her college friends. Maybe I would take her up on that. My nights alone were growing a little too long, and they could use a little light.

THE END

From the author

Thanks so much for taking the time to read *Cold Shadows*. If you enjoyed it, I hope you'll consider leaving a review of this book (or the first one!) at the retailer of your choice. Good reviews are possibly the most important factor in helping other readers discover a book.

The third book in the Ellie Jordan series is already in the works. I hope you'll continue the adventure when that book releases in February 2015!

Sign up for my newsletter to hear about my new books as they come out. You'll immediately get a free ebook of short stories just for signing up. The direct link is http://eepurl.com/mizJH, or you can find it on my website.

If you'd like to get in touch me, here are my links:

Website (www.jlbryanbooks.com)
Facebook (J. L. Bryan's Books)
Twitter (@jlbryanbooks)
Email (info@jlbryanbooks.com)

Thanks for reading!

Made in the USA
Lexington, KY
15 October 2016